ALEXAND

THE
STITCHWORT
CURSE

Cover illustration by Olia Muza
Interior illustrations by Alexandra Dawe

uclanpublishing

The Stitchwort Curse is a uclanpublishing book

First published in 2024 by
uclanpublishing
University of Central Lancashire
Preston, PR1 2HE, UK

978-1-916747-17-3

1 3 5 7 9 10 8 6 4 2

Set in 10/16pt Kingfisher by Becky Chilcott.

A CIP catalogue record for this book is available from the British Library.

Printed and bound in Great Britain by Clays Ltd, Elcograf S.p.A.

For Rowan, who read this first.

And for Jacob, who said he'd read it
'when it's a proper book'.

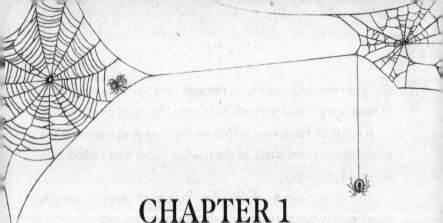

CHAPTER 1

ETTA PEERED THROUGH THE GAUZE VEIL, watching the hole in her bedroom ceiling growing wider.

'A little more please, nearly there,' she whispered gratefully to her tree.

She turned back to her nest-like bed and continued gathering pillows and cushions to add to the heap in the centre. Etta stood shakily on the pillow pile and reached up, fingertips stroking the intricate cobweb canopy draped across the ceiling of the tree hollow.

'I'm so sorry,' she whispered apologetically to the glowing spiders clustered in nooks and crannies all around the beech's hollow interior. They'd made an especially beautiful canopy for her this time; a pattern of snowflakes, each one unique and glimmering in the ghostly light from their soft bodies. Etta gently began to break through the curtain of webs until it fell loose and wafted down to her outstretched arms. Delicately she draped it across the twisted branches that circled her bed.

Looking up, Etta saw the hole she'd asked for in the ceiling was

1

likely big enough for her to fit through now. She adjusted the bag of tools slung across her back, then poked her head up through it.

It was pitch black, she couldn't see anything at all – unsurprising really, inside a tree trunk in the dead of night. Etta looked back down at her spiders.

'I could use some light for the climb to the top. Would you mind terribly coming with me?' she whispered politely.

After a heartbeat, they swarmed forwards, scuttling up the sides of her hollow tree bedroom and up into the darkness beyond. Etta waited patiently as they jostled each other a little, trying to get through – from tiny baby spiderlings to the fluffy adults, some of whom were bigger than her hands. She was able to tickle under their furry little chins and stroke their soft backs as they passed her.

Finally, enough had gone by for Etta to put her head and shoulders through the hole and look up. As the glowing spiders spiralled up the beech tree's interior, their light outlined the knots and whorls she could use as hand and footholds on the climb to the top.

With a relieved puff of breath, Etta sank gratefully down onto one of the large branches that burst through the roof of Stitchwort House, letting her clanking tool bag slip from her shoulder. A particularly fluffy spider dropped from the bough above to perch on her knee, preening and cleaning their adorable little face. They waved a leg at her in warning, so she hooked the bag's strap over a smaller branch for safety. Imagining the clatter the heavy tools would make if they slid down the roof and past her parents' bedroom made her shudder. Even worse, if she fell off and died trying to catch them, she'd never hear the end of it.

The slates were covered with thick snow, bright and sparkling in the moonlight, as though strewn with diamond dust. Even if she fell and slid off, there was probably enough fresh powder below to soften her landing. Although it might be best not to test that theory. Not with her own bones anyway, but there were enough skeletons around the house and grounds that she could conduct a few experiments before next time. That could be quite an interesting investigation and one that needed doing soon, before the snow melted.

If it ever melts.

Etta groaned as she hauled her tool bag back across her shoulders, then lifted the spider to rest on the strap. The weather at Stitchwort had been getting more and more intense over the years. After three months of it, Etta was a little tired of snow.

A nearby branch pulled her up to her feet and Etta began the slippery, treacherous walk across to the bat tower, her clutter of spiders keeping pace. The snow made the roof of Stitchwort appear smooth and pristine when it was anything but. Beneath the soft down of the powder duvet grew thick balls of moss to trip on; lurked cracked and broken tiles, and poorly patched holes just waiting for Etta to put her boot through.

The branches of her tree helped her balance as far as they could reach. Etta's tree was a twisting, curling beech more than a century old. It was a giant, stretching towards the ocean to the east, limbs curling away from the bat tower and the ruined west wing. All too soon, the last twig forlornly slipped from her grasp and Etta was alone, contemplating her choices beneath the bright moon.

That is the problem, Etta thought grimly as she gingerly prodded the smooth snow in front of her with the toe of her boot. *I don't have enough choices.*

She made it up the steep roof to the ridge tiles and began to balance along them, like a tightrope walker she'd seen in a book.

And they went across Niagara Falls – all I'm doing is walking on the roof of my own house. And that's all I'll ever get to do if I can't find a way out of here.

She gasped as her foot slid and she fell with her knees either side of the ridge. She caught the little spider as it tumbled from her shoulder and placed it on the snow as the rest of the clutter rippled with concern.

'I'm fine, I wasn't concentrating,' Etta murmured crossly as she got up, brushing the snow from her mittens. 'We're here now anyway.'

Laid out below Etta were the decaying remains of the west wing, ruined by a fire in Stitchwort's past. Family legend said the fire was set by angry faeries, Etta's father said possibly from a candle or maybe even lightning. Either way, Etta wasn't allowed in the west wing as it was 'structurally unsound', according to her family. It was one of the few places on earth Etta didn't really want to go. Everything in there was damp and mouldy and, despite being open to the elements, the west wing never manifested anything interesting to draw or study, like a nest of baby birds or a swarm of bees. It was thoroughly dead and dull.

But just at the corner of the main house, before you turned into the west wing, stood a partially ruined tower. Known to her family as the bat tower, for the bat roost it housed, it was one of Etta's favourite places to escape to. The crumbling walls were good for climbing as high as she could to see out of Stitchwort and away to the sea. Sometimes she might see a ship out there.

Etta knew all about life on a ship, she had read so many adventures in her ancestors' journals in the library. If she could ever manage to leave Stitchwort, Etta would fill her own journal and add her own story to the family archive.

I can't leave until I find a way around the curse though.

And that was why she was on the roof, in the wee small hours, with a bag of spanners.

Etta stepped down from the roof to the partially collapsed floor of the tower. She'd patched it up with pilfered floorboards until she could cross via safe walkways between the holes. The remains of the circular walls curled around her, the grey stone giving her secret workshop a little shelter from the elements as she walked to her workbench; she'd made it herself by butchering a wardrobe no one was going to miss from the servants' quarters.

Etta walked up the wooden steps she'd constructed out of old apple crates to the raised platform she'd made and checked inside the basket, just in case any wildlife had decided to move in. It was all clear, and she allowed herself a moment to admire her handiwork. She'd found the large wicker laundry hamper collapsing in an upper floor corner almost a year ago and had delightedly made it her secret den. It made an ideal spot to hide in when Grandmother was looking for help cleaning out the goats.

Then one day, while idly browsing for something new to read in the library, Etta had found a journal by Jacob Starling, who was visiting Paris when the first passenger balloon had taken flight. Jacob had carefully drawn the passengers: a sheep, a cockerel and a duck, all tucked up safely in the little basket. Etta had been rooted to the floor in the library; her eyes were fixed on the drawing of the balloon hovering above the crowd, but her mind hadn't stopped racing.

Every Starling outside Stitchwort had perished in the claws of the family curse, but what if she were able to live her life in the sky? Could the curse find her if she were amongst the clouds? Could Etta live her dream life as an explorer, a plant collector or a cartographer, like her ancestors? Eating and sleeping in the basket of the balloon, would she be safe as long as her feet never touched the ground?

For several months afterwards, Etta and her spiders had covertly worked to repair the basket, then moved it to her new secret workshop. The bat tower had the remnants of a floor still clinging on. With some quiet dismantling in long unused areas of Stitchwort, Etta had filled in the gaps with a mismatched assortment of old floorboards, borrowed wardrobe doors, drawer bottoms and even the seats of chairs. The spiders had helped with a rope bridge across to her working area, and, after a near miss, she'd added safety railings made of broken furniture and extra-strong spider silk. Then the hours and hours of spinning, weaving and sewing began.

Reaching the platform Etta gazed up at her balloon, a perfect white sphere, like a second moon, glowing pearl-like in the

radiance of the *actual* snow moon shining above. Etta quietly crossed to the storage trunk where she kept her notes. Below her platform slumbered the bat roost, hanging upside down all huddled together. They weren't due to wake from their hibernation for a few more weeks yet.

Inside the lid of the trunk, Etta had pinned posters of Sophie Blanchard, a pioneering female balloonist who Grandmother definitely wouldn't approve of. She'd also made a scrapbook of newspaper articles, pamphlets and prints about balloon flights and aeronauts, all collected by Jacob Starling. It appeared 'balloonmania' had swept across Europe and Jacob had been caught up in the excitement.

Lucky for me! Etta thought. *Although not so lucky for him.*[1]

Etta stroked the cover of her balloonist manual, made by painstakingly copying every scrap of information she could find in the Stitchwort library. It had taken a long time and she felt deservedly proud of it. Tonight was the next step of the operation.

Crouching to dig to the bottom of the trunk, Etta pulled out her research journal.

Finally, we can fly!

Opening her tool bag, Etta pulled out the length of rubber tube. It was old, and a little cracked, but it was exactly what she'd hoped to find while she'd been secretly scouring every dusty room in the house in her free moments.

---

1 Jacob Starling attended a balloon pyrotechnic display in Paris. Unfortunately, the balloon caught fire and descended rapidly upon the crowd, who were all able to flee except for Jacob, who was cornered by a stray rocket, preventing his escape.

'We're lucky to have had so many inventors and scientists in the family. Now we can start making the hydrogen!' she told the spiders, pulling on her goggles as they swarmed all over the balloon, checking their silk for even the tiniest of tears.

It was a freezing cold night, but a clear one. This was perfect weather for her first practice flight; she didn't want to be flying in poor visibility or high wind.

'But how long will it take to fill it up?' Etta wondered aloud. *I need to complete the tethered flight before anyone else wakes up.*

Etta huffed with frustration and glared down at the distant village. Who knew what wonders existed out there in the world by now, that could help her dreams of freedom become reality. All her research material was over a century old.

Nothing new ever happened at Stitchwort. Did the villagers ever look up at the wood on the hill and wonder about it? Probably not, the curse had wrapped the house in an invisible shroud, and the faerie woods had a fearful reputation. No one ever came up here. Stitchwort was lost and forgotten.

Nothing ever happens here, Etta thought gloomily.

All the spiders suddenly stilled. The skin on Etta's arms tightened into goosebumps and the back of her neck prickled.

Something isn't right . . . she thought, slowly standing as she let the rubber hose drop into the open trunk. Etta heard a low rumble in the distance. She looked up at the clear sky, frowning. *It isn't thunder.*

She held her breath and felt it again, a deep grumbling that travelled through her feet and into her belly. Pulling the goggles off, she squinted through the swallowing blackness beneath the trees surrounding Stitchwort. The noise was louder now – a low growl, punctured with uneven coughs.

Whatever it was, it was getting closer.

Etta half-turned towards her rope bridge, debating if it was foolish to wake her parents just to tell them she'd heard something strange, when there came a loud metallic clanging. The gates of Stitchwort were some distance away but the sound of them screeching as they were forced apart carried easily through the silent, snow-smothered night.

Etta gasped as the noise echoed around the tower. She clenched her fists, digging her fingernails into her palms as her blood pounded in her ears.

'There's no time . . .' she breathed. Etta ran back across the rope bridge, calling for the spiders to start spinning their fastest. She launched herself onto the steeply angled roof, skidded down in a flurry of snow and leapt off the edge.

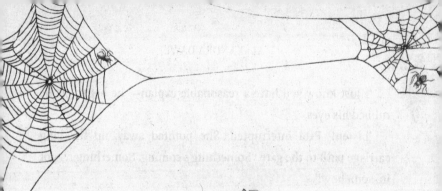

CHAPTER 2

ETTA THREW OUT HER ARMS ACROBATICALLY and grabbed the tree branch that whipped out from the eaves to catch her. The spiders were already spinning their fastest, a gleaming silver rope appearing before Etta's eyes even as her tree began lowering her. Etta caught the rope, secured it around the branch and quickly abseiled down to her parents' window, aware that the coughing and banging of whatever was coming their way was drawing closer.

Her heart pounded, and her sweating hands slipped on the silk as she scrambled down to the window that seemed further away than ever.

I think I'm panicking, she told her worried spiders. *Mother and Father will know what to do though.* Reaching the top of their window, Etta banged on the glass.

'Mother! Father!' she cried as she carried on down past it. A moment later, the window was flung open and her father, James Starling, looked up and all around before peering down at her.

'I just know you have a reasonable explan—' he began, as he rubbed his eyes.

'Listen!' Etta interrupted. She pointed away, up the long carriage path to the gate. 'Something's coming. Something ... got in, somehow!'

Father leaned out of the window, frowning as he peered into the frozen night. The rumbling growls shook the still air, louder and closer than ever.

Etta's mother, Mary, came to his side, already pulling on the old woollen military pelisse she used as a housecoat.

'It's not possible. Nothing and no one can get in,' she announced crisply, glaring out of the window as she tugged the fur-lined sleeves down.

Father reached out for Etta's rope.

'Quickest way to find out,' he remarked. He hooked the silk around his foot and offered Mother his arm, as though they were merely going for a stroll. The beech branch lowered them all swiftly, but gently, to the portico below.

'Etta, send the biggest spiders you can,' Father called, as he ran down the steps after Mother.

'I've already called them,' Etta replied irritably, following closely behind him.

Spiders were pouring from under the ivy that covered Stitchwort, and out of the cracks in the window frames. The larger ones would have to find another way through ...

She winced as she heard a crack of glass breaking.

Father turned around and grasped Etta by the shoulders.

'What are you doing? Get back inside! This could be dangerous, love.'

'I'm not a baby, I want to help! Where's Mother?' Etta cried as she tried to push past her father.

Her thumping heart felt like it was trying to escape her ribs, and her throat felt unusually tight. More loud rumbles came from the woods, almost immediately drowned out by the fracturing sound of tree roots tearing the frozen ground apart. Snow flurried and fell as the tree trunks began to move.

'Mary!' gasped Father. He spun Etta around and thrust her back towards the house, then ran away from her. He was swallowed by the shadowy gloom beneath the trees just before the thick trunks twisted together and closed across the path behind him.

Etta followed. She bypassed the wall of trunks by scrambling up the first tree she came to. While these trees weren't magical, like her beech, they were full of her spiders, who wove a glittering path for her across the boughs and pulled awkward branches out of her way as she sped past, following the sounds.

Etta nearly tumbled to the ground in disbelief when she caught up with her parents. Mother stood in the centre of the road; her splayed hands raised in the air. Behind her, a semicircle of trees were bowed down, branches woven together, making a barrier that had forced the intruder to a halt.

Father stood at her side, holding a heavy branch like a cudgel. In spite of his slippers and too-short pyjamas he looked formidable, but not as scary as Mother. Her face gleamed as white and cold as marble in the moonlight. Mother was glaring at the beast she'd trapped, flexing her fingers as she willed ivy to crawl down from the trees and oil across the forest floor to encircle the invader.

Easing herself down to a crouch, Etta silently studied the prisoner from above.

Surround it, she commanded the spiders, as more and more of them reached her. They moved out, silently filling every tree.

The trespassing thing was large, squat and shiny. At first, she thought it some kind of hard carapaced creature, but it had wheels like a carriage. Where she expected the beast's eyes was a rectangular window that reflected the starry sky above.

Its rumbles grew quieter, then it let out a final loud cough with a burst of noxious smoke from its nether parts.

Etta's ears rang in the sudden silence. The only sounds were her father's heavy breathing and the rustle of ivy tendrils as they wound themselves around the wheels of the beast, binding it to the floor. She tasted metal and dirt as the sting of the creature's alien smell reached her frozen nose.

With a squealing groan, a wing case stiffly opened out from the beast's body. No, not a wing case, Etta realised. A door.

It is a carriage!

She saw slim legs in trousers tentatively touch down upon the ivy-covered ground, the vines immediately wrapping around their ankles. They gasped and gripped the door with delicate, dark-skinned fingers as they gingerly stood. Mother swiftly sent ivy spiralling up to bind that hand tightly in place as well. A wide-eyed face peered fearfully around the door. Etta stared at this unfamiliar, new person.

She's very pretty, and riding in a strange carriage . . . is she one of the fae? Is this a new attack?

Father moved forwards slowly, lowering his weapon. He too stared openly at the first new face he'd seen in decades. The woman held up her other hand to stop him approaching and demanded,

'Blijf staan, alstublieft! Wie bent u?'

Definitely fae! Etta tensed, readying her spiders.

'English?' asked Father gently.

The woman moved to step out from behind the door, but Mother clenched her fists and the stranger cried out, falling to her knees as the ivy winding around her legs bound her tighter.

Etta scrambled to her feet in disbelief. Mother used her magic to grow food or to send weeds marching off the flowerbeds to a more suitable part of the garden. Etta hadn't ever considered that she could defend Stitchwort, bending trees to form barricades and binding intruders to the ground.

We must help! Etta told her spiders.

She crouched and stroked one of her biggest tarantulas, their legs spreading across two tree limbs. Concentrating, Etta felt in her mind for the connection to the rest of them.

Go, surround that woman, and her carriage!

In the darkness, Etta felt motion. Around her, branches creaked and shifted, soft flumps of snow quietly thudding to the ground as they unbowed from under the weight of the biggest and heaviest spiders at Stitchwort. Pumpkin-sized, they silently crawled down the trunks of the trees and joined her wolf spiders, surrounding the carriage while remaining in the shadows.

Etta could tell that the stranger knew something was there, her eyes darted about constantly, trying to keep track of the soft, furtive movements she could sense at the edge of the light. Her one free hand began to pull and tear frantically at her ivy bindings.

No, thought Etta, and in the shadows the spiders hissed a warning.

A cry came from inside the vehicle.

'Mama!'

A boy of maybe Etta's age scrambled out to tug helplessly at the strangling vines with his shaking hands. His sudden appearance alarmed Etta and several of her goliaths jerked forwards defensively, rearing up and chittering their enormous fangs threateningly. The woman's eyes widened, and she let out a small cry as she tried to shield the boy behind her.

Etta felt a tickle in her mind as a tremor ran through all of her spiders. Something about the boy . . .

Wait . . .

Father held up his hands.

'Everyone, calm down. Mary, wait. Stop.'

All around the clearing, spiders began to drop down from their branches like rain, creating a glowing dome over them all as they hung from a gossamer shower of silver silk strands. Before Etta's eyes, they hurriedly spun a single word that shone in the moonlight:

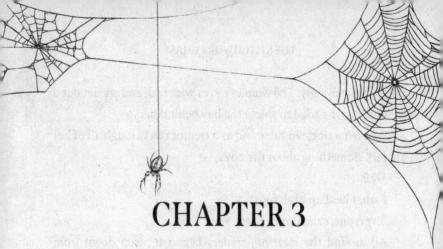

CHAPTER 3

THE IVY SLOWED ITS CREEPING ADVANCE BUT did not retreat. Everyone was still except the boy, trying to unwind the ivy from his mama's legs as she knelt on the frozen ground. A sob broke from him, and Mother looked away and down, relaxing her clenched fists. The ivy loosened and fell away.

The woman scrambled to her feet and backed up against the vehicle. She clutched the boy tightly against her.

'Please stop!' she called in accented English, her voice high and trembling. 'I'm sorry, we didn't know anyone was here.'

'Who are you?' Mother demanded. 'How did you get in here?'

'My name is Viola Grey.' She stepped forwards, holding her hands up. 'I'm sorry. I believed this house to be empty. I was not expecting to find anyone here.'

'It isn't empty. Please leave,' snapped Mother harshly. She stood straight and regal against the cold, her pelisse drawn tight around her, her expression as unfeeling as the busts lining the long gallery.

'Mother, no!' pleaded Etta, quickly swinging down on silver silk to join her parents.

Viola's face crumpled.

'Please, my husband, he's sick. We need a warm place, food . . .' Bright lines of tears ran down her cheeks, shining against her brown skin.

Etta's father looked at his wife.

'We could sort this out indoors, in the warm?' he suggested softly.

Mother stepped away from him.

'How did you get in?' she demanded. 'We don't go anywhere until you tell us how you know about this house. How you found it?'

Viola slid a large, old key on a chain out from under her clothes. She held it up for them to see.

'This belonged to my great-grandmother, Benita Starling. She lived here over a century ago.'

Mother's jaw sagged and the trees began twisting away, back to their rightful places.

'My . . . my great-grandmother was Benita Starling as well. You . . . you're family,' she breathed incredulously.

They stared at each other until the boy touched Viola's arm.

'Mama?' he whispered, shivering.

Viola looked up and around at the retreating trees and foliage.

'May I please drive closer to the house?' she asked nervously. Mother gave a terse nod, then turned and swept back up the driveway without looking back. Tucking his freezing hands under his armpits, Father turned to trudge after her. Viola glanced down at his worn slippers and bony, white ankles.

'Would you like to ride with us?' she asked. 'Felix can sit in the back with Ronald, my husband.'

Felix had been transfixed, staring at the dog-sized spiders prowling in the shadows. Hearing his name, he woke from his trance and quickly ran around to clamber into the back seat of the vehicle, which Father stared at with undisguised curiosity.

'Is it . . . an automobile?' he asked, tentatively poking at the hard shell of the beast. 'I saw one once, when I was a boy, although this one looks quite different.'

Viola laughed.

'It is an automobile, or a motor car, or just "car" is fine.' Viola looked at Etta with a small wave and a smile. 'Hello,' she said. 'Would you like to squash in the back with Felix?'

Etta stared at Viola, with her shiny automobile and pretty smile, wearing men's trousers. Her mouth dried up and her tongue stuck to her teeth. Etta shook her head and backed away until she could grab some trailing silk threads and hoist herself up into the trees again.

As Etta watched from high up, she saw her father getting into the motor car. There were two dull thuds as the doors slammed shut, then the beast coughed itself back to life again.

Mother was nowhere to be seen when Etta dropped to the snow-covered ground and ran up the front steps to the portico. Silently she sent her spiders back inside, out of the cold. Then Etta watched warily from behind a pillar as the automobile noisily grumbled its way up to the house, like an overgrown stag beetle looking for a fight. She could see Felix through one of the windows, his face pressed against the glass as he looked up at Stitchwort.

Father jumped out first, and hurried round with Viola to the back seat where a man lay under a blanket, barely conscious. Viola and Father helped him to his feet. Etta couldn't see his face as his head was hanging down. She frowned as he was not wearing a hat or coat in spite of the cold. Creeping down the steps to see better, Etta found herself edging up to Felix. She studied him openly for a moment.

His clothes were smart, but too small for him and poor for the winter. He was the opposite of herself; his skin warm brown earth where hers was cold white snow, his hair short, black and neat, her own a white mane of curls and tangles. Had Etta had the slightest inkling she'd meet strangers today she'd have unplaited the crow feathers and maybe even considered a comb.

Felix turned to catch her looking at him and they both glanced away immediately, cheeks heating up.

'I'm Etta,' she mumbled, hoping the night hid her red face.

'Felix,' the boy replied, his sad eyes returning to his father.

'Where have you come from?' Etta asked, astounded that they were here.

'The Netherlands,' Felix said, jamming his hands in his pockets.

Etta's eyes widened at the distance they'd travelled.

'You speak English though?'

Felix nodded.

'Papa is American. I speak English and Dutch. Mama too.' He smiled slightly. 'Mama learned English faster than Papa learned Dutch.'

'What's wrong with your father?'

'They took Papa, to ask questions. He came back sick.'

'Who took him?'

The man supported between her father and Viola was a wasted skeleton who could barely lift one foot to put before the other. Etta had never seen anyone this ill before. Viola was murmuring quietly to him in a language Etta didn't know.

'What sort of questions?'

'It don't matter,' he replied, finally looking at her again. 'No one ever get the right answers. Not if you black, or Jewish, or they think you in the resistance.'

'But who are "they"?' Etta almost howled with frustration.

'The Boots, the Nazis,' Felix said, exasperated, as if that explained everything. Before Etta could question him further, Viola stopped.

'We use this door?' she asked, pointing at the front door of Stitchwort.

Father shook his head.

'It's locked, the key is lost. We'll go in via the kitchen door, it's around the back. Bit of a walk I'm afraid, and your car won't fit through the side gate.'

Viola pulled the black key out again. She darted past Etta and Felix and up to the huge oak door. With a little difficulty, she forced the heavy key into the ancient lock and turned it round with both hands. The whole house seemed to shiver as the lock grudgingly clunked free. Squealing like a beansidhe,[2] the door complained loudly as she shunted it open. Viola turned and grinned at their shocked faces.

'This will be quicker? *Ja?*'

Felix didn't make it very far into the hall before his legs faltered and his jaw dropped open. Etta walked straight into him, but he was so busy staring that he didn't even notice.

As the door hadn't been used in countless years, all manner of household clutter had accumulated around it. Beyond the junk was an incredible sight. An enormous tree was growing in the middle of the hallway – its trunk touching the walls in places – huge, thick branches reaching up and through the ceiling. It had absorbed the elegantly curved staircase that had once stood as the focal point of the entrance, the steps becoming part of the tree.

---

2 A beansidhe (ban-sith, ben shee or banshee) is a faery that sits on the roof, shrieking and wailing, when there has been, or is about to be, a death in the household. They make a truly dreadful sound.

The reaching branches were swathed in spiderwebs, hung with witch bottles and spell bags, some painted with curious runes. There were birds' nests, pairs of shoes stuffed in a nook, a teapot resting at a precarious angle halfway up the banister, a scarf and hat dangling from a convenient twig, even a cricket bat lying across a low branch.

'Mama and I saw the branches coming through the roof,' Felix said quietly to Etta. 'We thought it would be cold inside, and soaking wet. How do you live here? I thought you were ghosts at first!' He huffed a small laugh as he turned to look at Etta.

Etta had been watching her father helping Viola across the hall with her husband. Viola's clothes were so different from what the Starlings wore; everything from the stitching to the way they fitted looked new and exciting to Etta.

She felt Felix's curious gaze, and her skin prickled under her Victorian nightgown. The old lace shone white in the moonlight, like her hair, both enhanced by the faintly glowing spiders that accompanied her everywhere. Etta wondered if she really looked like a ghost haunting this strange old ruin. Before Etta could reassure Felix that the house was dry, mostly, and she was absolutely alive, Father called from the top of the kitchen stairs.

'Come on, you two. Let's get warm and have something to eat.'

Etta cupped the face of a nearby spider; they were all silently waiting around the hall, watching Felix.

'False alarm, but thank you!' she called. She flashed a bright grin at Felix and impulsively grabbed his hand. 'Come on!' she burst out. Then, without another word or a backwards glance, Etta ran down the stairs, dragging the startled boy in her wake.

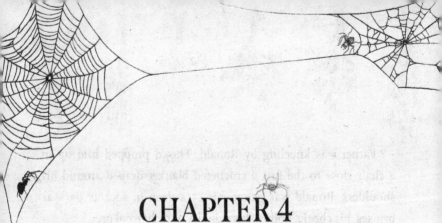

CHAPTER 4

ETTA QUICKLY SAT IN HER USUAL SPOT AT
the dining table. She was fizzing like sherbet, as though it
were her birthday or Christmas.

Nothing ever happens at Stitchwort – never, ever!

This was the most exciting day of her predictable life.

Felix hovered near the low kitchen doorway, as though he
might bolt back up the stairs at any moment. Eyes wide, he took in
the kitchen: the ancient, scrubbed dining table under small, high
windows, surrounded by mismatched chairs, the vast black range,
a deep inglenook fireplace where the fire was filling the room with
the scent of woodsmoke, and the battered workbench in the centre,
pale in the middle where Etta's father kneaded bread dough daily.

This solid worktable had been built in the kitchen and
was as old as the house. It was scarred from centuries of cooks'
chopping, with pots of utensils clustered at the edges and buckets
of vegetables on the floor at the sides. Pans and bunches of drying
herbs hung from the beams above. Etta heard Felix's stomach
moan at the sight of so much food.

Father was kneeling by Ronald. They'd propped him up in a chair close to the fire, a crocheted blanket draped around his shoulders. Ronald was gaunt, his eyes deep in sockets dark as bruises, his cheeks hollow, his skin dry and charcoal grey.

'I'll wake my mother, she'll brew up a tonic,' Mother murmured to Father as she slipped her boots off.

Father got to his feet and helped Viola up.

'Tea,' he stated firmly. 'We need tea, and breakfast.'

Etta felt suddenly shy as Viola sat at the table. She hid behind her coils of white hair as she took secretive peeps at her.

In the golden light of the kitchen Viola's bronze skin glowed. Her black hair was roughly bound under a scarf and her brown eyes were red-rimmed. Viola's thin hands were shaking slightly, and she placed them on her lap to disguise the tremors. Etta wanted to look under the table to see her trousers. Trousers! On a lady!

What will Grandmother make of that? thought Etta, hiding a mischievous grin.

The Grey family's clothes were worn, but Etta could see they were good quality. The growing lamplight revealed they were neatly, expertly mended. Everyone at Stitchwort was terrible at mending. Most of their salvaged, mismatched clothes had ungainly patches and lines of spidersilk stitches wandering like silver ants across them.

'Felix?'

Viola held out her hand and he scurried across the kitchen like a timid mouse to cling at her side. He slid into the chair next to Viola, huddling close, his eyes round as he stared at Etta's father.

Etta considered her father through a stranger's eyes. His large, freckled hands were purple with cold, his hair wild from sleep, not yet neatly parted and combed down, and his beard was as fluffy as a badger's bottom.

No wonder they're staring! she thought, biting the insides of her cheeks to stifle a snort.

Unconcerned, Father was lifting down his gleaming copper pans and fetching a wooden spoon and a whisk to make pancakes.

Pancakes, thought Etta dreamily. *We haven't had pancakes for months! Having visitors is wonderful!*

Viola and Felix were astounded when breakfast was served.

There was steaming hot porridge with honey from the Stitchwort bees, eggs any way you liked (Felix enormously enjoyed his dippy eggs with thick toasty soldiers), rich buttery pancakes, two huge pots of tea, creamy milk, butter and cheese from the goats. Plates were passed up and down the table, the jam spoon got stuck to Etta's elbow and three butter knives clattered to the floor in the confusion.

'Zijn hier geen voedselbonnen?' Felix asked Viola as he helped himself to another slice of cheese.

'English, darling,' Viola said quietly to him. 'My apologies, we haven't seen this much food in a long time. Felix asked if there's no rationing here,' she explained to everyone.

'What's rationing?' Etta asked curiously, but no one heard her over the clamour of dishes.

After a slice of plain toast and a black tea, Grandmother bent over Ronald, frowning with pursed lips as she looked into his eyes and ears. Felix chewed his lip as he watched, squeezing Viola's hand.

'Etta,' said Mother quietly. 'Why don't you show Felix the library. He can rest there a while.'

'They're getting rid of us so they can talk without us listening,' grumbled Etta darkly in the hall. 'I bet they don't tell us anything about Great-great-grandmother Benita.'

She turned to see why Felix wasn't answering, to find him staggering slowly up the kitchen steps groaning and holding his stomach.

'You only ate half of what I did!' exclaimed Etta, amused as she watched him.

'I'm not used to it!' Felix puffed as he caught up. 'I don't remember when we last had a proper hot meal!' He groaned and rubbed his tummy again.

'Why on earth not . . . ?' Etta began as she ducked under a low branch and heaved open one of the tall library doors. She fell quiet when she saw Felix's reverent face as he stepped through. He stared up at the thousands of dark shelves tiered from floor to high ceiling. The early dawn light gleamed golden through the glass dome in the roof, making the brass fittings shine.

The library was a warm, round room, three storeys high, with a great spiral staircase running from bottom to top, and galleries that ran all the way around the second and third floors. There were spindly ladders on rails for reaching books on high shelves, and a colossal desk with a captain's chair, with doors behind to the gardens.

Clustered around the fireplace were mismatched Chesterfields, small tables, and a once beautiful, but now rather shabby, Persian rug. There was a basket of lumpy knitting beside one sofa and a pile of mending heaped on another. Etta inhaled deeply the glorious aroma of leather, old books, woodsmoke and something deep and sweet – treacle or chocolate maybe. She noticed as Felix spied the last three slices of rich, dark fruitcake under a glass dome. There were lamps on the walls, and portraits of Starlings gone by smiled down at them.

Felix turned, entranced, to the nearest shelf of books. They were world mythologies, exquisitely illustrated.

'You can look at any of the shelves down here,' Etta told him, as she piled up kindling in the grate. 'But the higher up you go,' she pointed up towards the top floor, 'the more dangerous the books get.'

'Dangerous?' Felix asked, startled.

'Oh yes, books can be very dangerous,' she replied matter-of-factly, standing up to light a lamp.

'Wait, you must cover the windows!' Felix exclaimed, horrified.

Etta looked at him in surprise.

'Why would we need to?'

'Verduisteren!'[3] Felix shouted in panic, running to the garden doors. 'You have no blackout curtains!' he called incredulously as he staggered back from the window. 'Quick!' he shouted and dived under the desk.

Etta calmly finished lighting the lamps and the library brightened in their honey glow. She walked over and bent to look under the desk. Felix was huddled cross-legged underneath, shaking, his arms tight around his body.

'Are all boys like this?' she asked curiously. 'I haven't met one before.'

Felix didn't respond at first, his eyes focused upwards, surveying a sky miles above the underside of the desk. Then he looked at her, his face scrunched up in confusion.

'You never have visitors before?'

Etta laughed, then stopped awkwardly when she realised

---

3 'The Darkening' is the name for the blackout imposed on the Netherlands by the invading Germans, to make it harder for Allied bombers to navigate to Germany.

Felix wasn't joking. She crouched down to his level.

'Of course not. The family curse . . .? You know about that, don't you?'

Felix looked at Etta blankly.

'The house is hidden,' she explained slowly. 'So, no one ever visits. And if we leave, we'll die, probably in a freak accident of some kind – that's our family curse. So I've never seen a person who wasn't my parents or grandparents, except for portraits. You're the first new people I've ever seen!'

Felix unfolded his arms from around his knees and leaned forwards.

'You telling me a curse killed all the people in our family?' His whole expression was disbelieving, even scornful. 'If that were true, how would my mama, papa and I be alive?'

The library door opened. Etta stood to see her father and Viola supporting Ronald as he shuffled into the library, Mother behind them carrying a bundle of blankets. They made up a sofa into a bed for Ronald, then Viola and Mother arranged blankets and pillows on two of the library daybeds.

'Felix,' Viola called gently, as though shivering under tables was an everyday occurrence. 'Felix, come here, we need to get some rest now.'

'Etta?' Her parents called her over quietly and she slipped from the library. Etta paused in the hallway, still puzzling over Felix's question.

How had *the Greys survived the family curse?*

CHAPTER 5

'FINALLY!' ETTA EXCLAIMED FROM HER REGAL position reclining on a thick bough over the stairs. She closed her book and surveyed Felix through narrowed eyes. 'Are you actually allowed out now? I've been waiting forever,' she grumbled.

Felix grinned up at her. It was the first real smile she'd seen from him. Already his eyes were brighter, and his cheeks were filling out.

'It was only a few days! We caught up on lots of sleep, and unpacked, and your parents keep bringing in food, blankets and firewood. And your Grandmama keeps giving us different tonics.' He paused. 'She's a bit frightening?'

'Goodness, yes,' agreed Etta, putting her book over a branch before jumping down. 'She's particularly good with birds as well, unfortunately,' she muttered as she rearranged her skirts. The spiders shivered at

the mention of 'birds' and drew further back into the dark crevices of the hall.

'Well, now that you're finally released, there's something I want to show you,' Etta announced.

Felix skipped over a root and followed her up the stairs, then down a long, dim hallway lined with paintings so dingy and brown you could barely make out what they were paintings of.

Etta stopped and beamed at him as she threw open a door that led into utter darkness. She nudged Felix ahead of her, then left him stumbling, arms outstretched, as she navigated her way to the window.

There was a soft thump, and Felix's muffled voice came from much closer to the floor.

'Show me what?' he groaned.

Etta stood before the tall window, concentrating with furrowed brows as she directed several spiders. They scuttled up, down and across the velvet curtains, spinning a gleaming thread. Etta turned her hands palm up and raised them. As she did, the spiders heaved and the drapes pulled away from each other and up, allowing the snow-bright daylight to slice into the room.

'Swell,' Felix murmured flatly, kneeling up while looking around the room, flurries of disturbed dust swirling in the light that streamed in.

The room smelled old and lonely. Neglected furniture stood between haphazard heaps of forsaken belongings. Buried under piles of discarded clothes was a beautifully carved four-poster bed. The floor was a mess of scattered trunks, boxes and books.

'Why'd you bring me here?' Felix asked, looking around blankly.

'This room is along the hall from mine!' Etta burst out, opening her arms wide in triumph. 'If we're quick, we can claim it as your bedroom!'

Felix looked at the tattered remains of a broken umbrella crumpled on the floor, its ribs folded in like the curled legs of a dead spider. He shuddered, his eyes travelling across the dusty heaps swagged with thick cobwebs.

'You're expecting there to be a queue for it?' he asked, eyebrows raised.

'I know it's a bit messy now,' Etta started, standing on one leg as she tried to find somewhere to put her other foot. 'But Father always says many hands make light work, usually on wash day. And each of *our* helpers has eight hands!'

Felix flinched as the wolf spiders trotted into the bedroom, using the walls as well as the floor. Etta tensed, then cleared her throat.

'I'm sorry we scared you when you arrived. We had no way of knowing you were family. It really is a marvel that you're alive at all,' she said wonderingly.

'It sure is,' Felix agreed fervently. 'We've been on the run for months.' He took a longer look at the bed, his shoulders losing some tension. 'It'll be nice to have a bed that's mine again, even if it is covered in old socks.'

'Tell me about the war, and the outside world, and all your adventures!' Etta asked as she started flicking through some of the books.

Felix tugged the tattered drapes from around the bed, dust and debris cascading down all over him.

'Curse first,' he coughed. 'Whose is all this rubbish anyway?'

'It is not rubbish!' Etta retorted hotly. 'This all belonged to Elizabeth Starling.' She held open a journal to show Felix the detailed paintings inside. 'She was a phytologist.'

'I don't know that word,' said Felix, shaking the thick cobwebs from his black hair.

'A botanist? A plant scientist; she studied plants, before she disappeared.'[4] Etta indicated the books and drawings that surrounded her. 'These will have been hers.'

'Did she disappear so she didn't have to clean her bedroom?' Felix jumped quickly out of the way of the largest wolf spider, with sandy brown fur and black stripes, carrying a bundle of books strapped to its back with silk.

'Oh, the mess isn't her fault,' Etta said, holding out the next pile of books to another spider. She smiled and stroked the top of

---

4 Elizabeth Starling 1765–1818. Brought a rare Cobra Lily back to Stitchwort after her last expedition but disappeared in the Poison Garden. The Cobra Lily has thrived phenomenally though.

their head. 'That's it, slip them in on the second floor of the library. Don't let Grandfather see you.'

She turned back to Felix.

'When someone in our family dies, everything they owned sort of rains down inside the house. We believe it's part of the curse, removing every trace of the Starling line from the outside world.'

'This curse again! Who cursed us?' Felix asked, his arms wide. 'And why?'

'Those are the great family mysteries!' Etta replied, sorting items into piles. 'We know the curse was cast in 1818.'

Felix laughed. 'That's over one hundred and twenty years ago. Someone would have told me, if it was true! You're making up stories to tease me!' He threw the string of pearls he was holding onto the jewellery pile, rubbing the cobwebs off his hands as he turned away.

'That's why we were so confused when you turned up!' Etta exclaimed. 'We didn't know anyone else was still alive, we thought it was just the five of us left. Everyone else in the entire family has died!'

'So how are you and I here? We should never have been born,' Felix argued, holding his head upside down and trying to ruffle the cobwebs from his hair.

Etta rifled through a torn book, searching for a blank page.

'Our great-great-grandmother Benita Starling escaped from the fire that ruined the west wing of Stitchwort. Her brother Edgar tragically lost his life, trying to save her. Benita fled to relatives in the Netherlands,' explained Etta.

'When she got there, Benita was put in an asylum for "hysteria", because she said faeries had attacked Stitchwort. We've several family letters from back then, where everyone was gossiping about it.' She arched an eyebrow at Felix. 'Then letters start coming in saying "have you heard about cousin Henry", or "Great-aunt Enid", as everyone started dying.'

'Last week, in the library, you said they died in strange ways, freak accidents?' Felix queried.

Etta nodded.

'There are journal entries and newspaper clippings, obituaries and things, as well as the letters. Grandfather and I put together a whole curse timeline, using all the evidence.'

Felix shoved his hands deep in his pockets and paced the area of floor they'd managed to clear. 'So, Benita was in the asylum insisting the household was attacked and cursed by faeries, and you have letters and articles reporting unusual deaths in the family. Putting those together you believe we really are cursed by the fae?'

Etta nodded and started writing names on the page, drawing spidery lines between them.

'Benita eventually married and had three sons. One of them went travelling and never returned, one came here to Stitchwort, my great-grandfather, and the other stayed in the Netherlands and was your great-grandfather.' She presented Felix with the quick family tree she'd drawn.

'Stitchwort is protected somehow,' she continued, as Felix rubbed at his neck and hands. 'We're safe in here. I think Benita's big brother, Edgar, sacrificed his life to help her escape. I also think he protected the family home with his dying breath, else the whole lot would have burned, not just the west wing.

'He was a wonderful artist, scientist and inventor, as well,' Etta finished smugly.

'What about my great-grandfather? He wasn't protected in the Netherlands,' Felix pointed out, still trying to pick long, sticky cobwebs off his sleeves.

'Yes, I've been wondering about that . . .' Etta tapped the book absently with her pencil. 'It could be that Edgar was able to extend his protection spell over his sister somehow, which protected her children,' she mused. 'Or maybe he gave her something, some talisman that kept her and her descendants safe?'

'Like the Stitchwort door key?' Felix asked.

'That might be it!' Etta cried delightedly. 'It could be the key, and it's been passed down through the generations, keeping you safe somehow. Hmm . . .' Etta scribbled something down and tore the page from the ruined book, folding it and slipping it into her pocket. 'That's given me an idea for a little project I have.'

Felix grinned. 'So, it's a good thing we came, and brought the key; you should have been delighted to see us! Not tying your first visitors up and threatening them with giant spiders.'

'They're not even that big!' Etta patted the back of a wolf spider as it trotted past. She didn't even have to bend down to run her fingers through the long hairs on its back. 'My father first came here because he was lost, he stumbled into our orchards. My mother took fright and had all the apple trees throw their fruit at him. It took ages for Grandmother to heal him, by the end of which he liked Mother so much he decided never to leave!

'You remained conscious the whole time, there's not even a scratch on you! It really could have been much worse.'

'Your father is not affected by the curse?' Felix asked curiously, still feverishly rubbing at his hand where the cobwebs had touched him.

'Not then. Mother says it was quite useful for a time. Grand-mother sent him to the village with money to buy supplies, but after he started stepping out with my mother, he had several near misses and they decided it was too risky to continue.'

'You've really never left this house? You don't know anything about the world?' Felix's eyes bulged out in a manner Etta found somewhat insulting.

'I've been in the garden!' Etta retorted indignantly. 'It's a big garden, acres of it. There's the kitchen garden too, and orchards and woods. I climb the trees and look over the wall. I've seen the sea and . . . and boats! There are thousands of books here – I know about history, geography, economics, science and art . . . and everything!'

'Just nothing after 1818 . . .' Felix murmured, his eyes so full of pity that Etta stamped her foot crossly.

The wolf spiders stopped what they were doing and faced Felix, who backed away against the cobwebbed bed, feeling their eyes on him.

'That's not true,' Etta glowered, her brown eyes darkening even more. 'I told you, everybody didn't die immediately. It took years, we had a big family once. More books and things arrived for a while. My grandmother knew some things when she arrived, and my father did actually go to school.'

Felix wasn't listening anymore. His hands were covering his face, scratching at the dirty strands of web that clung to him. He was mumbling something too quiet for Etta to hear. Etta tilted her head, trying to catch what he was saying, and all the spiders in the room mirrored her movement. She stepped forwards and reached out tentatively.

'Felix?' she asked, as the wolf spiders closed around them, each with eight bright, berry-black eyes fixed upon the boy.

Felix shivered and cried out, rubbing his hands and hair where the tattered drapes fluttered against him, dropping more dirt onto him.

'Get them off me,' he begged. Etta quickly grabbed an old stocking from the bed and began to gently clean the rest of the cobwebs away.

'What's happening, Felix?' she asked softly.

CHAPTER 6

'I, I DON'T KNOW,' FELIX MUMBLED, WRAPPING his arms around his sides. 'I felt all itchy and tingly with the dirt all over me, it got stronger and stronger. Then . . .' he shook his head, looking down at his boots. 'I don't know,' he sighed. 'It's all confused.'

'Can I get you anything? Maybe it's too soon for you to be out of the infirmary. I can fetch my grandmother?' Etta fretted.

'No!' Felix said quickly. 'I feel better now. I just . . . I thought I heard a voice, a woman. I felt cold, and strange. And sort of . . . squeezed?'

'Squeezed?' Etta asked, looking at the too-large, borrowed jumper that hung loosely on Felix's small frame.

'Is that the word? Squozen? Squashed?' He shrugged. 'It's gone now. I just heard a woman speaking and I felt like I couldn't breathe.' He shuddered, rubbing at his arms as though the sticky residue from the cobwebs was still clinging to him. 'It was pretty awful.'

Etta closed her eyes and zipped through the eyes of her

favourite spiders, the ones she had the closest connection to.

'There's no one else up here, Felix, just us. You can't have heard voices, unless . . .' She jumped up with excitement. 'Ooh, maybe you can talk to spiders too!' She beckoned a wolf closer and took hold of Felix's hand.

'Look deeply into her eyes,' Etta braced herself as Felix recoiled from the spider. 'Can you hear her?' she asked firmly.

Felix shook his head very fast as he pushed himself further back on the bed. 'No, no definitely not,' he stuttered rapidly.

Etta sighed and the wolf stepped back, stroking her feelers across her furry face.

'What's she saying?' asked Felix shakily.

'She was wondering if you'd miss one of your little fingers. She's terribly hungry and would like a snack,' Etta said calmly as she smoothed her skirts.

Felix gasped and quickly put his hands behind his back.

'I'm teasing, silly. She wants to know where she's taking all those underpants.' Etta thought for a moment. 'Mother said we were never to use the Limoges china again, after the chicken tea party incident. It's all boxed away in the butler's pantry. Pop all the bloomers in there. It'll be years before anyone notices.'

The spider obediently padded away and Etta turned her attention back to Felix.

'What is your gift then?' she asked, sitting on the bed and swinging her legs. 'What can you do?'

Felix sat down beside her.

'What do you mean?'

'What are you drawn to? What . . .' she paused, looking for

the right word. 'What calls to you? When you talk, what listens? Mother can order plants around, like she orders me around! Father can do amazing things with food, like bake a birthday cake that'll guarantee you'll have the best day ever. Grandmother has a way with animals. Even the bees don't sting her when she takes honey, but birds are her favourite. They'll perch on her arms and eat from her hands. Grandfather's an artist, a writer and an excellent historian. And I have an affinity with spiders. I can connect with them.'

Felix smiled weakly.

'Yes, I had wondered about that.'

'So . . .' Etta lightly prodded Felix's shoulder. 'What can you do?'

Felix opened and closed his mouth silently.

'Er . . . I don't know. Nothing,' he shrugged helplessly.

'Nonsense, Felix, you're from a long line of inventors, artists and scientists. Creativity is in your blood; how do you channel it?' She paused, giving him a chance to respond. 'What do your parents do?'

Felix tugged his jumper sleeves down over his hands.

'Mama makes costumes for the theatre, and the cinema. Her costumes are up there on the silver screen. That's how she met my dad. He's a jazz musician,' Felix said proudly.

'What's jazz? And the silver screen?' Etta began, then held up a hand. 'No, I'm getting distracted again. You'll have to explain that later. But your parents are both creative, they make music and costumes. That's their magic.'

Felix pulled a face.

'That's not magic. That's sewing, which is slow and boring.

43

I have to help Mama sort her threads sometimes, it takes forever. Then music, that takes hours and hours of practice. It's not . . .' He wiggled his fingers in the air. '*Poof!* Magic!'

Etta stared at him.

'Who said magic was easy? You still have to study, and work, it takes dedication. It's exactly the same as drawing or learning a musical instrument, it's all about practice. Music turns your emotions around, costumes are part of the illusion being woven around the audience, immersing them in the story. It becomes real to them. They both cast a spell. With their abilities, your parents are telling a story, changing reality. That's magic.'

She looked around the room.

'Now they're here at Stitchwort, their talents will grow even more. That happened to my father and grandmother. The house is drenched in old magic from generations of Starlings spellcasting here, it enhances everything. That's why the spiders are so big and live so long. Cobwebs just soak up magic, like plants soak up sunshine. Spiders sit in the webs, some even eat their old webs when they want to spin new ones, so they ingest the magic.'

'That doesn't explain what just happened to me though. That voice.' Felix frowned down at his hand, still rubbing it.

Etta couldn't explain it either.

'You heard a voice, but everyone's downstairs and it wasn't the spiders. Maybe you do have a gift, but you don't know it yet?' She sighed. 'Another mystery. We do seem to collect them here.'

Lost in her spinning thoughts, Etta's gaze drifted across the room. It already looked much better and was going to be a lovely bedroom.

Under the dust was a deep, forest-green carpet, patterned with scrolling foliage. The moss-coloured velvet curtains at the tall windows were heavy and thick. Exotic patterns of leaves, birds and monkeys covered the walls, giving the feeling of being in a lush rainforest. There was a large fireplace with a threadbare armchair to one side. If she added a deep rug and some cushions it would be a cosy place for Felix to read.

'It's a bit bare, isn't it?' Etta asked Felix, her hands on her hips. 'I know!' She spun around. 'We'll go up to the attic and you can look at my old toys, see if there's anything that you'd like. Come on!' And she ushered Felix from the room.

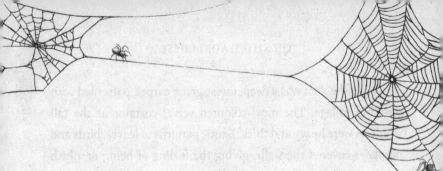

CHAPTER 7

ETTA CLOSED HER EYES, SCANNING THE house. She frowned, turning slowly. 'Let's just see . . . Grandfather's reading in the herbarium, your papa's sleeping in the infirmary . . . where are they? Oh!'

She ran down the hall and opened a window. They both shivered as chilly air swept in. Etta pointed across to the vegetable beds in front of the greenhouses where her parents, Viola and Grandmother seemed to be having a disagreement with some very large plants. Etta rummaged in her pockets and pulled out a pair of opera glasses.

'Oh dear,' she said with feigned sadness, holding them out for Felix. 'I don't think Mother's had enough rest since she moved all those trees. I'd warrant Father's been badgering her for extra vegetables and Grandmother will want medicinal herbs for your papa as well. The strain has brought on an attack of her nerves, she's lost control of her magic. Now last year's runner beans are back. Such a pity.' She grinned brightly at Felix. 'I do like to know where they all are, so I can be sure they're too busy to come looking for me.'

Felix held the glasses up to his eyes just as an overgrown bean pod burst open, showering the garden in red, spotted beans the size of dinner plates. One hit Etta's father in the stomach, sending him to his knees.

'We'll be eating beans for months!' Felix cried mournfully.

Etta shook her head and pointed.

'The chickens are coming to our rescue. They'll eat anything, and they don't listen to Grandmother!' She closed the window with a rebellious cackle as the bean plant sent out tendrils as thick as Felix's arm to anchor itself defiantly onto the garden wall.

Etta and Felix ventured up the cramped, narrow staircase to the attic door. There was an uncomfortable, prickly feeling as Etta shunted it open, as though they'd interrupted a conversation and everyone had turned to stare at them. There was no one there of course, just piles of old furniture and trunks, hammocks of cobwebs, books, ephemera and the dry smell of old dust. Dim light splintered through small, oddly spaced windows and lit up swirling dust motes.

Immediately by the door were a few boxes with Etta's old things in them: a wooden boat, carved by her grandfather; a pretty painted music box; a box of dominoes; some carved animals which weren't strictly speaking toys, but were so lifelike and enchanting that Etta had begged to be allowed to play with them years ago. Felix was delighted with it all.

Etta's eyes gleamed as she surveyed the further corners of the attic that she'd never been allowed to explore. Mother and Father were irrationally against Etta poking about in the attic alone, just because of a rumour about a painting that ate people,[5] a missing trunk of poisons and all the traps hanging from the ceiling and walls.

'Let's have a look around,' Etta suggested. 'We might find more things you like.' She tipped out a nearby basket and headed towards a cluttered bookcase, filling her basket with anything that looked interesting along the way: polished stones and pale shells, a fine pocket-knife with a mother-of-pearl handle, a compass in a leather case.

Felix caught up and stayed close to her. Every time they caught movement out of the corner of their eyes or waves of goosebumps prickled along their skin, he would jump and get so close to Etta they'd bump heads or knock knees. There was nearly always a reasonable explanation for the movement – once a mouse, another time an enormous brown spider.

'It's probably hunting the mouse; we've never had a mouse problem,' Etta confided.

They saw shadowy cobwebs wafting on breezes they couldn't feel. Disturbed dust motes swirled, even in parts of the attic they hadn't been near yet. Felix trod on Etta's heels again and she finally exploded.

'Is this what having friends is like? Can't you give me just enough space to breathe, please?!' she fumed.

'Sorry,' Felix said sheepishly, his head down and his shoulders

---

5 Several staff members had gone missing in the past when Stitchwort *had* staff. Etta often thought it would be helpful to know what it was actually a painting *of*.

hunched. 'I don't like it up here. It's like the bedroom downstairs, but worse. I feel . . .' He shuddered and looked at Etta pleadingly. 'I feel itchy and tingly. Like there's something all over me.'

'Have you heard any voices at all?' Etta asked.

Felix shook his head.

'It's probably because it's so dusty up here and you're used to being clean then,' Etta reassured him. 'We'll look around a bit more before we go.' She headed determinedly for a crowded bookcase pushed against a wall, beyond which was the next section of the attic. Pausing at the bookcase, Etta's eye caught a glimmer in the darkness beyond, and she peered at it curiously. She looked behind to check Felix was still with her. He was nearby, holding himself tightly as his eyes darted everywhere. Etta sighed and put her basket down.

'Is it getting worse?' she asked. Felix nodded glumly. 'Can you hear voices?'

Felix shook his head, looking at her sorrowfully through his thick lashes.

'Hmm.' Etta studied Felix thoughtfully. 'It might be that you've had too much excitement after all you've been through, and you should be tucked up in bed with a camomile tea.'

Felix pulled a disgusted face.

'Or,' Etta suggested, holding out her hands, fingers outstretched. 'Your hidden powers are awakening in the magical miasma of Stitchwort!' She wiggled her fingers, laughing and making ghostly *woooooh* noises.

Felix gave a faint smile, then shivered. Etta dropped her hands to her sides.

'Felix, we can go downstairs now if you want,' Etta offered. She cast a longing glance over her shoulder at the promising glints in the darkness. She turned back to Felix, who was looking through the brick arch as well.

'You want to see what's through there?' he asked, pointing.

'Another time,' said Etta dismissively, holding out her arm to lead him out of the attic. Felix linked his arm with hers, then spun her around so they were both facing the gloomy arch.

'Just a quick look,' he said firmly. 'I feel gunky up here, like I need ten baths!'

Etta grinned and they stepped into the darkest part of the attic. They groped around dusty wooden crates and cracked leather cases until they reached a round table, shrouded in heavy, dark webs, so thick they looked like tattered fabric. Through the layers Etta could make out dark glimmers and glows.

Is it jewels? she thought. *Or treasure?!*

Etta grabbed the thick webs and tore through them, throwing them behind her, making Felix howl and jump away.

'What? Did a spider bite you?' Etta quickly checked the floor. Felix had his hands over his ears and his eyes squeezed shut. Etta gently patted his elbow, picking a long strand of black cobweb off his sleeve as she did.

'Felix? Felix?'

He opened one eye, squinting at her.

'What's the matter?' she asked.

'Can't you hear him?' Felix whispered.

'Hear who?' Etta looked behind her but couldn't see anyone nearby.

'I don't know,' hissed Felix, both eyes open and frantically darting about. 'I heard a man,' he moaned.

Etta slowly turned a full circle, holding her breath so she could listen out for the smallest of sounds.

'I can't hear anything,' she whispered. 'Is the voice near or far?'

Felix's cold hand gripped hers, she could feel him trembling.

'Listen!' he insisted, squeezing Etta's hand until it hurt. Pins and needles prickled her fingers where they interlaced with his, and the dark, dusty cobweb twined about their hands, binding them together.

Etta felt a strange cold sensation start to spread beneath her skin, unfamiliar and nauseating.

'It's all around us,' Felix whispered close to her ear. Suddenly Etta felt a voice slithering through her brain like a tentacle, leaving her feeling cold and slimy.

Help me.

'Ugh!' she shuddered, pushing herself away from Felix, shaking the cobweb off. 'That was horrible, right inside my head.'

'Yes!' cried Felix. 'You heard it too?'

'Did it say, "help me"?' Etta hissed urgently, stepping closer.

Felix shivered. 'He's cold, and it hurts, I think.' He looked at Etta seriously, his eyes so wide she could see the white all the way around. 'Etta, is it a ghost?'

'I don't know,' Etta whispered honestly. 'I've never seen or heard a ghost in my life.'

'Are you not scared?' Felix asked. 'I don't like this. I've got tingles and goosebumps, and my head is . . .' He paused, shaking his head, as though trying to clear water from his ears. 'I feel strange.'

Etta looked at him through narrowed eyes.

'I've never felt like that, and I've never heard a voice in my head like that before.' She paused. 'Maybe this is your talent? Maybe you're a person who can talk to ghosts?'

'But you heard it too,' Felix pointed out. 'It's not just me.'

'That's true.' Etta's mind raced, then she grabbed Felix's hand and gripped it tight. 'You held my hand!' she said, speaking quickly. 'Earlier, you were scared, and you squeezed my hand and then I could hear it too!'

Felix yanked his hand back, but Etta held on stubbornly, feeling that creeping, cold sensation spreading between them again as the cobweb suddenly slithered, binding wrist to wrist.

Felix stepped backwards and through an old tennis racquet, losing his balance and sitting heavily down into a box, pulling Etta with him. As she fell her arm caught on one of the thickest, darkest webs that trailed from the beams around them.

Etta felt her feet leave the ground, the black cobweb swirling around her like a ragged ribbon. Felix tried to pull her back down, but he was lifted up too.

They floated higher, speechless, as the black cobweb drew the other trailing webs into orbit around them. The dark webs encircled Etta and Felix like a flock of tattered crows, moving faster and faster, pulling them along. Etta felt like she was drowning, being tossed and tumbled around as though in a swift river.

She managed to grab Felix's jumper as he was flung past her. She spat hair out of her mouth and tried to speak. One look at his face told Etta that Felix was in difficulty as well. His eyes rolled and he clutched at her.

The black spiderwebs eddied around them, writhing and spreading like ink. Darker shapes began to form within, coiling and twisting, moving with the flow.

CHAPTER 8

ETTA GRABBED FELIX'S FACE WITH HER HANDS, forcing him to look at her.

'The webs, I think it's coming from them,' she choked out, as the cobwebs swirled around them. 'Grab the cobwebs! Tear them down!'

She let go of Felix and kicked her legs, like her parents had taught her in the pond every summer.

Etta swiped her hand and grabbed a handful of black cobweb. It was repellent, oily and greasy on her fingers. The web squirmed, like a live grub, but she forced herself to hold on. Next to her she saw Felix snatching at the spiderwebs as well, bundling them up in his hands.

The dark shapes that had formed were looking more solid now, and long too, some longer than Etta was tall. They slipped and swam through the swirling chaos sinuously. Etta could feel a pressure building on her skin. She felt heavy, and her hair was lifting like it did before a thunderstorm broke, even the hairs on her arms.

One of the shapes swam under her, then rolled and twisted, surrounding her like a corkscrew. Etta saw a blunt, featureless face, the same shape as her mother's shovel, and felt the gaze of its cold, pale eyes. Its belly was pale too, and the darker skin on its back was pocked with rows of deep indentations.

'Eel!' Etta called in warning to Felix, wherever he was. 'Don't touch them!' she gasped, tasting river sludge on her tongue. But it was too late, Felix's brows were lowered as he took aim and kicked out at the eel surrounding Etta. Its head snatched back, blue lines crackled along the length of its body and out into the spinning cobwebs, flaring them up from within like lightning in a towering thundercloud.

Electric eels.

Felix yelled as the cobalt blue discharge lurched across his boot and up his trouser leg.

'Don't touch them!' Etta repeated, not sure if he'd heard her. The eel was no longer surrounding her, but Etta could see the growing outlines of more building. She grabbed another fistful of spiderweb, crushing it into her hand. The ball crackled with little blue sparks; they nipped like ant bites.

'Hurry!' Etta cried, as flickering blue light told her another eel had discharged a shock. 'I think they were inside the cobwebs, but they're coming out, and getting stronger!'

As Etta reached for another handful of swirling webs, she saw a man's face spin by, with round cheeks and a moustache as fluffy as a tarantula's knees.

Help me.

She felt the words in her head, slippery as soap.

'Where are you?' Etta shouted, trying to swim back to him against the current. 'What's happening?'

Instead, she found Felix, his elbow crashing hard into her nose, sending a wave of hot pain bursting across her face.

'This is ridiculous!' Etta yelled, suddenly furious. She tore vengefully at the cobwebs, even grabbing a thrashing eel by the tail. The electric bursts hit like wasp stings and her hand spasmed with the pain, but Etta clung on determinedly and squashed the eel down into her fist. It fragmented as she crushed it, falling back into dirty, oily webs.

'They're not real, Felix!' she shouted, her foot grazing a tabletop as she was swept by, fighting for control.

Etta looked around quickly. She and Felix each had sizeable clumps of cobweb in their fists, there was much less of it encircling them now. The maelstrom was losing its power as they gathered the webs.

Felix pushed his bundle into her hands and grabbed the last eel around the throat, gritting his teeth as it shocked him. He wrestled it into the wad of webs, pushing every last bit down inside.

Holding it all together, Etta could feel the pressure within, blue lightning crawling all over the ball as pins and needles inched from her fingertips to her elbows. Etta held the ball in her outstretched arms as it spun her around. Felix swirled around her, trying to reach the last ribbon of cobweb as it danced just out of his reach.

'Got it!' he yelled triumphantly and began stuffing the length of it into Etta's hands. The face appeared again, floating between them – sorrowful eyes with bushy brows and a huge moustache – translucent and faded like an old watercolour.

Help me . . . he moaned, the words trickling like a cold drip inside their heads.

Horrified, Etta hurled the whole sticky mess away from them as hard as she could. The bundle flew across the attic, deeper into the darkness, the blue sparks illuminating weird shapes of abandoned possessions, before it splatted into a chimney breast and collapsed.

As soon as Etta threw the ball away, she and Felix fell, landing on top of an old cupboard.

'What . . .' Felix paused and started again. 'What just . . . what was that? *Who* was that man?'

Etta lay beside him, staring at the damp patches on the attic ceiling.

'I have no idea,' she said slowly. 'It was certainly new to me.'

She sat up and swung her legs over the side of the cupboard, looking for a way down. In the shadows below was the round table they'd been investigating earlier. It was covered in strange ornaments, but there were gaps in between for their feet.

'This way,' Etta said, using the doorknobs as footholds.

The table wobbled as Etta stepped onto it, and she stumbled into Felix, following close behind. They both fell forwards, landing painfully on their hands and knees as the table swayed.

Then, from beneath them, came thuds, as the things on the table began to fall to the floor. Etta grabbed one of the smooth, slick lumps before it fell. They reminded her of apples in cold storage.

'Crystal balls!' she announced, as realisation dawned. 'The whole table's covered in crystal balls!'

'And we've knocked the stands over.' Felix winced, as every time they moved, more crystals started to topple and roll towards the table's edge. They tried to stop them, but their hands and arms filled up and the cascade of tumbling crystals kept flowing to the ground around them. As each one left the binding properties of its stand it began to wake up, the crystals' magic activating.

'Bother,' grumbled Etta, as a purple crystal began to glow brightly and levitate out of her arms.

Felix quickly scrambled off the table, tripping over the shiny balls and their elaborate stands. A vivid, poison-green ball started to smoke, singeing one of the many rugs laid out over the attic floor. A black crystal was spinning very fast and Felix quickly put his left foot on top to hold it still.

'Etta, what do we do?' he asked.

A huge, pearly white crystal was heading determinedly away from them, moving with purpose around any obstacle in its path. Nearby an oily-looking, malevolent red one was emitting a high-pitched whine, while a huge ball filled with swirling ultramarine smoke was bouncing up and down on a bedframe.

'Catch them!' Etta ordered as she jumped from the table. 'Catch them and match them back up to the right stand.'

Felix grabbed a bonnet from an open drawer behind him. Swinging the bonnet by its ribbons he scooped up the red crystal that was creating such a commotion. As soon as it was matched up to the correct stand the noise stopped, and the red glow subsided.

Etta grasped a pair of tongs from a nearby fireside set and passed Felix a butterfly net. Etta began to stalk the green ball across smouldering rugs. Felix pounced on another ball, trapping it under his net. It dragged him across the floor, bunching up all the rugs as it ploughed relentlessly onward.

'We're doing well!' Etta panted to Felix after another twenty minutes had passed. She wiped her brow. 'We've got most of them now, I think.'

'When you've quite finished patting yourselves on the back, would you care to explain what you think you're doing up here and why that rug is on fire?' came Mother's dangerously quiet voice.

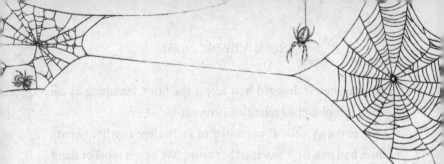

CHAPTER 9

'I THOUGHT YOUR GRANDMAMA WAS SCARY,' Felix whispered as they climbed up the kitchen steps after a very frosty dinner. 'But now I think maybe your mama is more terrifying.'

Etta waved a hand airily.

'She's just in a temper because she lost control of her magic and had a ridiculous fight against a beanstalk.'

When she found them in the attic, Mother had been livid that the children were 'messing about with things they didn't understand', and had 'nearly burnt what was left of the house down'. She'd been paler than usual, her chestnut hair in disarray, a bruise on her cheek and a fat lip. Her hands and arms were stained with soil and sap, and the bean tendrils' grip had left livid red welts on her limbs.

'We're lucky she didn't arrive any sooner and see the rest of it!' Felix groused. He stopped and looked at Etta seriously. 'You should have told me. You should have said you weren't allowed into the attic. You got me in trouble *and* I was absolutely terrified up there.'

Etta turned to face him.

'I'm not allowed in the attic *alone*. But I wasn't alone, I had you with me. It's not my fault they changed the rules. Anyway, how am I supposed to explain where you're not allowed to go if I don't show you first?' she finished reasonably, turning back and heading for the staircase.

'No, wait.' Felix jogged to catch up. 'That doesn't ... It sounds logical, but I don't think it works.'

Etta climbed the stairs breezily, throwing her words defiantly over her shoulder.

'It was an exciting adventure; we don't get many of those around here. We survived! Now, would you like to see my bedroom?'

Felix eagerly followed Etta to where a huge section of tree trunk bulged out across two-thirds of the wide hallway.

Etta placed her hand on a whorl in the bark and it began to untwist and open for her. Pale lavender light shone out through the widening gap.

They slipped inside, the trunk closing seamlessly behind them.

Etta smiled as Felix stood in the middle of the floor marvelling at her room. It gave her a funny, warm feeling to introduce her tree to someone else.

'This is where you sleep?' Felix exclaimed, turning a full circle. 'When I first saw the branches through the roof, I thought no one could live here – but you're here, inside the tree!'

Etta grinned, her cheeks and ears feeling hot.

'This tree and I are good friends. They started to open that knot hole for me when I was little. I played in here and asked the spiders to bring me cakes. Eventually I moved in.' She grinned mischievously. 'It doesn't open for Mother or Father at all, which drives Mother absolutely wild! She can't work out how the tree defies her!'

Etta pointed up to what looked like a tangle of twisted branches above them.

'Let's go upstairs.'

'I'm happy to hide in here all night,' Felix agreed fervently, as Etta climbed a silvery, silken ladder up to her sleeping platform. 'Anywhere I'm not getting ragged on by parents!'

Felix followed, the ladder swaying rhythmically with his movements. At the top, it was like a huge bird's nest. In the centre was an untidy tangle of blankets and pillows. All around were patched cushions and old toys. The undulating walls of the tree cradling them were full of nooks and crannies which Etta had stuffed with books and treasures. She showed Felix her favourite feathers, bones and pebbles; her sketches and stories, and her secret biscuit stash.

Sitting on her round bed felt like being inside a glittering magpie nest. Spiders roamed freely, moving points of light in the deep recesses, creating the soft lilac glow which lit the room, and cobwebs fluttered all around. Felix breathed in the pleasing scent of old books and gazed up at the gauzy canopy of snowflakes the spiders had woven, creating the feeling of a magical tent. The low winter sun spilled in through the tiny window, golden light drenching dozens of twinkling ornaments suspended from the ceiling. Dazzling rainbows slid along the walls; there were bright flashes of ruby and gold. Felix lay across

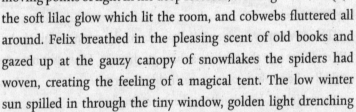

the bed and peered out at the trinkets as they gently rotated.

'What is all that?' he wondered aloud.

'That's an earring I found.' Etta pointed at a hanging glass teardrop. 'It's probably a diamond as it makes the best rainbows. There are old keys, feathers, a gold ring, a locket that doesn't open, an emerald hatpin, beads . . . The spiders bring them for me, because they're pretty I suppose.'

'I love it!' Felix burst out joyfully. 'I love your room, it's just . . . I love it. I couldn't love it more, it's perfect!'

'Now,' said Etta, sitting up with a notebook and pencil. 'I think we need to talk about what happened today. In the bedroom, and the attic. You heard voices! And did we see a ghost?'

'We need to talk about this curse first,' Felix sat up and folded his arms around his knees. 'Now that we're here, can we never leave again? Because, well, we can't stay forever! My papa's a famous musician. He's got a career, and family back home in America. He's going to take us on tour!'

Etta's shoulders slumped down, and she leaned back against the wall.

'I'm sorry, Felix, but I don't know what would happen if you left. You might have a terrible and ridiculous accident. I didn't question it while I was little, but a few years ago I began asking if we could visit some of the places I've read about, only to find out we can't leave because of the curse. Since then, I've been studying my ancestors' diaries, correspondence and journals. One will end abruptly, then I might find a

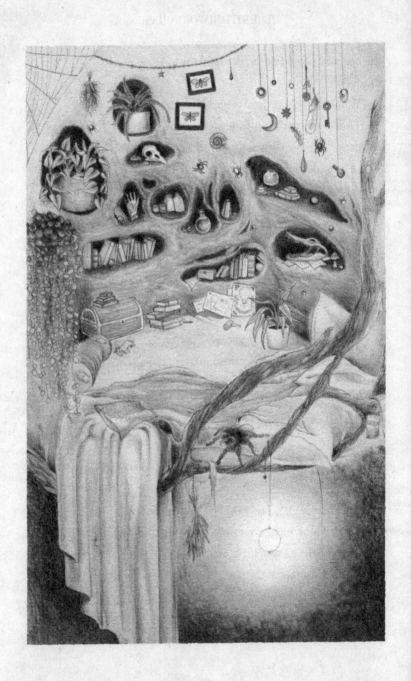

letter from one Starling to another telling of their death, and I can put the pieces together.' She put her head on one side as a dimly remembered something tickled her brain.

'Is something wrong?' Felix asked.

Etta shook her head, as though trying to dislodge a few spiders.

'Something's on the tip of my brain . . .' She waved a hand. 'It'll come back to me. What were we talking about?'

'How we're going to go travelling around America with my papa and his jazz band!' Felix reminded her.

'Yes!' Etta leaned forwards eagerly, clutching her pencil. 'I've been wondering how you've managed to evade the curse. Could the key really give you that much protection? How can one key protect three people?'

'Mama didn't carry the key with her either,' Felix said. 'She kept it in a drawer.' He looked down at his hands, as his voice dropped. 'In her bedroom, she had a dressing table. She always had flowers on it.' He sighed. 'I wonder if our house is still there now.'

Etta was staring at Felix.

'What sort of flowers?' she asked. 'It could be important – certain plants give protection. And stones too! Yes! Does your mama wear any jewellery?'

'Er . . . yes,' Felix answered slowly. 'It's all old though, I think . . .' He looked up, eyes bright. 'She said it belonged to her great-grandmother. And she said I should wear this always, for luck.' Felix pulled a gold chain from his pocket, with a heavy watch on the end. 'It was her great-grandfather's.'

Etta seized the watch, looking at it closely as she tilted it to catch the light.

'These black stones set around the case?' She held it out to Felix, pointing. 'These are probably obsidian, or black tourmaline. They're protective stones.' She turned the watch over and traced the design on the back. 'It needs cleaning to see for sure, but I think this engraving is a shield knot.' With a tiny click, Etta opened the watch case and peered inside. 'I need more light, please,' she murmured. Spiders began dropping around her, suspended on threads so their glow illuminated the inside of the case. 'That's strange.' Etta looked up at Felix. 'There's spider silk stuffed into the workings.'

Felix laughed.

'I'm not surprised. There are spiders everywhere in our house. *Were* spiders,' he amended. 'I hope they escaped, if anything happened to the house.'

'I thought you didn't like spiders?' Etta asked, a little accusingly.

'I don't like the enormous ones you scared us with outside,' Felix clarified. 'I don't mind normal ones, but you got too many here. We had spiders at home, but not like this. Mama was always complaining about cobwebs – not so many as you have though.' He pointed, laughing, at the cobwebs trailing like bunting around the interior of the tree.

Etta didn't reply, she was too busy scribbling in her notebook.

'Do you know if Benita Starling lived in that house?' she asked.

Felix nodded firmly. 'She did. There's a portrait of her in the hall with her husband. She looked like you. Same white hair, but her eyes were blue. He looked like my mama.'

Etta looked down at her notes.

'To recap, I believe Edgar rescued his sister from the fire – a fire I think was started by the fae, who then cursed our family for reasons unknown. Benita went to relatives in the Netherlands. Somehow, she was safe from the curse there, as were all her descendants. You all lived in her house, you had the Stitchwort door key, the house is full of spiders, you all have old jewellery of hers and your watch is full of cobwebs.' Etta looked at him seriously. 'Felix, these are all clues, huge clues, to how the curse works. Edgar must have somehow given his sister the same protection from the curse that Stitchwort has! What happened today – the voices, the cobwebs – that must be part of it as well.' Etta was growing more and more excited. 'Felix!' She jumped up, sending glowing spiders scurrying around the gnarled walls. 'Do you realise what this means?'

'No,' said Felix blankly as she handed back his watch.

'I'll need to amend my design.' Etta was pacing. 'I've been so busy considering the weight, the lift, the strength of the silk, I hadn't even considered other methods of protection. This could be the solution!

'If we figure out how Benita Starling was protected from the curse, we can recreate that protection for ourselves! Crystals and herbs, sewn into clothes and the canopy! Or maybe it has to be something belonging to Benita Starling, maybe her personal possessions could be some sort of talisman! We must run experiments!'

Felix lay down and fluffed his pillow. He yawned ostentatiously. 'When you've decided to let me in on the conversation, you just let me know,' he said, his eyes closed.

Etta yanked the blanket off him and threw it over the railings.

'Get your slippers on and get ready to climb!' she told him, before reaching up to tear through the silken canopy above.

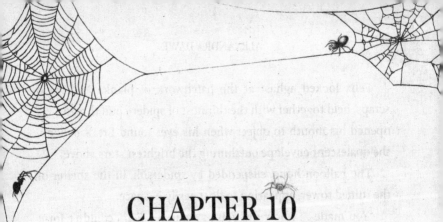

CHAPTER 10

'I'M SURE, IF WE'RE NOT ALLOWED IN THE ATTIC then we are *definitely* not allowed on the roof,' Felix snapped, his usually soft voice as crisp and angry as the biting cold.

'I'm sure if you were quicker, we wouldn't still be on the roof,' Etta replied scathingly, as she waited for Felix to catch up.

Felix's nose was so close to the roof tiles Etta could barely hear him.

'If I slip off, I'll die. Who would have thought my own cousin more dangerous than an actual war?'

Etta huffed out a frozen breath, and watched it fade into the night.

'I have you completely surrounded by spiders, you know,' she remarked.

'Is that supposed to be reassuring?' came the muffled reply as Felix inched forwards, his hands and knees gripping either side of the ridge tiles. 'It is not.'

Etta put out a hand to stop him before he crawled into her.

'We're here!' she said gleefully. 'There's a nice, sturdy floor to walk on now.'

Felix looked aghast at the patchwork of planks and wood scraps, held together with the thinnest of spider-spun threads. He opened his mouth to object when his eyes found Etta's balloon, the opalescent envelope outshining the brightest stars above.

The balloon hung, suspended by spidersilk, in the shelter of the ruined tower, appearing to float easily in space.

'You made . . . how did you . . . you . . .' Felix couldn't form a coherent sentence in English and muttered in Dutch under his breath.

'Do you like it?' Etta asked uncertainly. *After all, Felix arrived in a motor car. Perhaps my balloon is positively mundane compared to what exists outside?*

'I can't believe you made this!' Felix exclaimed, hurrying closer without a thought for the wobbly floor. 'I have a book where the characters steal a balloon and escape to a mysterious island.' He grinned at her. 'You'd like it. They do all kinds of science to make tools and inventions. You must read it!'

Etta smiled back.

'I'd love to,' she said gratefully. 'How did the people in your book get their balloon to fly?'

'It was filled with hydrogen gas, like a zeppelin,' Felix answered absently, as he leaned over the basket to look up inside. 'It's so beautiful! I can see how all the silk threads are woven together. It's magical!'

'What's a zeppelin?' Etta asked, reaching for her notebook and pencil. 'Am I spelling it right?'

Felix took the pencil and drew a long shape across both pages.

'These are the engines, and these are rudders and fins at the back. People travelled in a room underneath, just here.' He added some trees and houses at the bottom of the page so that Etta could see just how big it was.

'People are out there now, travelling about in these?' Etta marvelled.

Felix's face turned serious. 'There was a terrible accident with the hydrogen gas; one caught fire and crashed horribly. Lots of people died, it was awful. Papa says they won't be used anymore, hydrogen is too dangerous.'

Etta was hastily scribbling notes.

'That's unfortunate, I was going to fill my balloon with hydrogen.' She tapped the pencil against her teeth.

'What about hot air?' asked Felix. 'That's the other way of doing it. Heat . . .' he said wistfully, wrapping his arms tightly around himself.

'Would that work?' Etta asked, surprised. 'It's definitely worth experimenting with.' She made a note with her pencil. 'We also need to research protective crystals and plants, and how much they'll add to the weight. Maybe we could distil the herbs and rub the basket with a solution. Hmm . . .' she continued, furiously scribbling while muttering to herself.

'Can I sit in the basket?' Felix asked, leaning so far in his toes left the ground.

'Yes, good idea,' Etta replied, hopping in after him. 'There's blankets in the supplies box.'

'It feels like we're really flying,' said Felix happily, looking up at the brilliant moon from the swaying basket. 'Can I quiz you about the curse?'

Etta sighed and put down her sketches.

'You can ask anything you like, but I might not be able to answer.'

'Tell me more about Edgar and Benita Starling.'

Etta shifted to get more comfortable.

'Their parents were away a lot, cartographers you see. They were tragically lost at sea while Edgar was still a young man. He took over the running of the house and estate. From what I've read, he was quite wonderful – a society gentleman, witty and popular. Everyone wanted to be seen with him.' Etta beamed, imagining her great-great-uncle mingling at balls and high-society events. 'Edgar was also an exceptional artist and scholar; everyone was always congratulating him on his wonderful scientific drawings and discoveries.'

'Can I see them?' Felix asked.

Etta pulled a face.

'I can't find them!' she almost wailed. 'There's nothing in the library or any of the bedrooms. All the information I have is from other people's letters and journals, nothing from Edgar himself.' She sighed. 'I think his rooms must have been in the ruined wing. It's absolutely infuriating! I'd love to see his work.'

'You said something about faeries before, that you believe faeries cursed us?' asked Felix.

Etta nodded. 'Yes! What do you know about the fae?'

Felix shrugged, looking down at his slippers. 'They're secretive, they stay hidden. Not many people see them. Some people believe they've died out, or never existed at all.'

'What do you believe?' Etta asked, her eyes fixed on Felix.

He was quiet for a few seconds, still looking at his feet. Then he cleared his throat.

'I've never seen a faery. I . . . I always wanted to believe but I was scared people would think me silly or childish. There were faery photographs in the newspapers years ago, before I was born. Some people believed they were real, others didn't.'

He looked up and met Etta's gaze.

'After everything I've seen here, I believe.'

'Good,' Etta grinned. 'In that case, I'll tell you everything I know.

'A letter came to Stitchwort addressed to Edgar Starling, telling him his sister had arrived safely in the Netherlands and expressing concern for Edgar's welfare. They said Benita was extremely distressed. A following letter said they were forced to hospitalise Benita for "hysterics", and it was clear that Edgar had not replied to the first letter.'

'Did you find these letters?' Felix asked.

Etta shook her head.

'My grandfather did. You know Benita married and had three sons, two of them were our great-grandfathers. Cyril Starling, my great-grandfather, came to Stitchwort with his wife, looking for the answers his mother never gave him. He found piles and piles of unopened letters all over the place.'

'Benita didn't tell her children what happened here, all those years ago?' Felix asked, shocked.

Etta shook her head firmly.

'Grandfather says Cyril knew absolutely nothing about his mother's young life in England, he only knew her life in the Netherlands after she had children. Maybe she was afraid of being

ALEXANDRA DAWE

locked up in an asylum again, so she never spoke of her past. It does sound rather far-fetched, doesn't it?' She paused, her eyes huge and dark. 'Imagine. "Faeries attacked my house, burnt it down and did away with my brother!"'

'Is that really what you think happened?' Felix looked on the verge of laughter. 'You cannot believe that.'

'Ha!' Etta thumped the floor of the basket, causing it to bob about. 'There are things you don't know! From the evidence, Edgar Starling had a remarkably close relationship with the fae. His notes and drawings were of the most wonderful discoveries, that people had never heard of before. I don't know what happened but I wonder if he took it too far, if there were things he shouldn't have found out, or secrets he wasn't supposed to write down. I think the fae set fire to the house to burn it all, even though he was inside with his little sister!'

Felix scoffed. 'You have no proof of that! No proof the fae have ever done anything against this family.'

Etta folded her arms and leaned back against the woven willow walls of the basket. 'I do,' she said, slightly smug. 'My grandfather had a sister. You didn't know that, did you?'

Felix shook his head slowly.

'Myrtle Starling was his older sister, and she went missing one morning, from this very house, almost sixty years ago. Never to be seen again.'

'How does that prove the fae had anything to do with it?' asked Felix.

'Think about it,' Etta said. 'No one can see the house; Edgar's spell hides it. So, no one could have got in and kidnapped her.

74

She wouldn't have left, it's certain death out there for a Starling. Myrtle and my grandfather were very close; he's always insisted that she would never have left him. He remembers she liked to go out walking early to pick fresh flowers for the kitchen table. It's obvious! Myrtle was walking alone, she probably stepped into a faery ring or something and got whisked away.'

'Never to be seen again?' whispered Felix, transfixed. 'I had no idea.'

Etta nodded solemnly.

'My grandfather absolutely hates faeries, as you can imagine. Grandfather and Grandmother blame everything on faeries. They say they send us troubles, like plagues of pests all over the veggies. Sometimes Grandmother complains they've curdled her potions when they don't cure right, and she insists the fae and their curse are responsible for the awful weather we have. It gets worse every year!

'Every spring it rains harder, for longer; the roof leaks, bits of the house fall off, the garden floods then the vegetables rot. Right now, everything's frozen solid, I've never seen snow like this, neither's Mother, and she's never left Stitchwort either. It's too dry in the summer, everything wilts and scorches when the ground cracks. We're always racing around bodging and mending . . .'

Etta paused, looking intently at Felix.

'I'm not scaring you, am I? I didn't mean to make it sound dreadful here!'

'Not at all,' replied Felix. 'You don't know what it's like outside these walls right now. There's more food here than I've seen in forever, and you're safe!'

'Safe?' Etta laughed, without humour. 'Don't think that, not in this house. A housemaid died here once, tidying a collection of walking sticks. One was carved into a snake.' Warming to her tale, Etta lowered her voice and hissed. 'As she polished it, the stick came to life, swallowed her whole and then went back to being a stick again. It's still upstairs, you can see the huge bulge in the middle. I'll show you tomorrow!'

'What else can you show me?' asked Felix eagerly.

'I'll tell you all the best stories I've ever read in our families' diaries!' Etta promised, encouraged by his wide-eyed attention. 'Shipwrecks and crocodiles, poison, monkeys, espionage and everything!'

They stayed there, wrapped in blankets beneath the twinkling stars, whispering stories. Lulled by the gentle swaying of the balloon, neither of them noticed the other falling asleep.

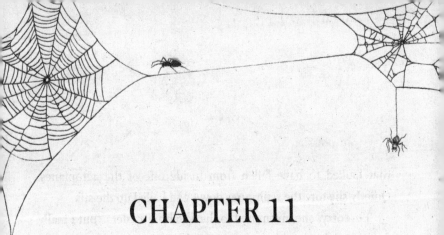

CHAPTER 11

ETTA OPENED HER EYES. HER BEDROOM WAS dimly lit by weak, winter morning light. She and Felix were curled in a tangle of blankets in her round bed, spider-spun shapes floating all around them, phantom sculptures from their dreams.

Kneeling up, she gently followed the contours of the unfamiliar forms suspended from the ceiling with her fingers. Great flying machines. Felix had spoken of them in the darkness last night. Flying machines that could drop death and destruction on hundreds, even thousands, of people. She remembered their names – awful, beastly names: Goblin, Demon, Fury, Meteor, Hellcat.

Etta shivered as she looked at Felix, still sleeping, his black hair vivid against the white pillow. The flying beasts spiralled down towards him, getting smaller and smaller as though they'd been spun right out of his dreams.

Nightmares she reminded herself.

Etta reached out and broke the thread of an ominous shape

that looked to have fallen from inside one of the aeroplanes. Quietly she tore the sculptures down and balled up the silk.

'I'm sorry,' she murmured to the watching spiders. 'But I really don't think he should see this sort of thing when he wakes up.' She listened for a moment. 'I don't understand war either.'

Etta looked over at Felix again, a thick woollen blanket pulled right up to his ears. She smiled as she thought of his reaction last night to her spiders spinning a thick candyfloss covering over them both in the balloon, to protect them from the spreading frost. Felix had been . . . perturbed at being tucked in by quite so many legs and had insisted on climbing back down to Etta's bedroom immediately. He hadn't even stopped to pick up his slippers.

'That's it!' Etta gasped. 'Felix, Felix!' She kicked out her feet where they met his in the centre. 'Felix, wake up!'

He sat bolt upright in shock. '*Is het een luchtaanval?*'

'What?' Etta glared at him. 'Listen! I've had an epiphany!'

Felix rubbed his hand over his face and squinted at her sleepily. 'What?'

'She locked the door,' Etta said breathlessly.

Felix looked blank, then yawned expansively. 'What time is it? Do you think your father will be making breakfast yet?' He stretched, then saw Etta staring at him expectantly. 'Who? Door? What door?'

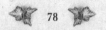 78

'The front door of Stitchwort. Benita Starling locked it and took the key with her.'

Felix waited, trying to look patient and not like he was thinking of homemade jam and crumpets.

Etta didn't say anything else, continuing to stare at him intently.

'Erm, yes? She did?' He agreed, failing to keep the question from his voice.

Etta leaned forwards, wrapping her arms around her knees.

'Don't you think that's rather strange? The house is burning and her brother's presumably trying desperately to control the fire, helping her escape. And she stops to lock the front door? With him still inside!'

Felix paused, trying to imagine the scene. He rubbed his head.

'We locked our door as we were leaving, to try and stop, er . . . *plunderaars*? I don't know what you would say, like pirates or thieves?'

'Looters,' Etta replied. 'Opportunistic thieves.'

'Exactly,' Felix said. 'Some people boarded up windows as well, hoping their houses would be untouched when this is over.'

Etta shook her head.

'No, your escape was planned. I know you didn't have a lot of time, but it's not like how quickly you'd leave if the house was on fire.'

'True,' Felix considered for a moment. 'If the house was on fire,

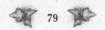

locking the door would be pointless. The windows are all gone! Anyone can just climb inside.' He wrapped the blanket more tightly around himself. 'Maybe it was the fright of the situation, just doing things the way she always did?'

'You think she locked the door out of habit?' Etta frowned, pushing her blankets aside. 'I don't know, I think there's more to it than that. We don't really know anything about her.' She took a deep breath. 'What if she killed him?'

Felix snorted. His laughter trailed off awkwardly when Etta didn't join in. 'You're not serious?'

Etta nodded slowly, climbing down the ladder while working through it aloud.

'Maybe Benita killed her brother somehow. Poison maybe, or, I don't know, pushed him down the stairs? Then she set the house on fire to cover the evidence, locked up and calmly walked out of here.'

'I thought he was this absolutely wonderful gentleman that everyone adored?'

'Quite,' Etta reasoned, looking for a matching stocking on her jumbled floor. 'He was brilliant, witty, clever, popular, talented. He'd inherited Stitchwort, and all of their parents' money. There's hardly a mention of Benita in any of the journals or letters I've found. "A very quiet and reclusive girl" is about as descriptive as it gets! Maybe she was riddled with jealousy? Secretly plotting her brother's murder so that she could have all the money and attention!'

'But she didn't get all the money,' Felix pointed out, leaning over the railings. 'She was hysterical when she arrived in the

Netherlands and was put in an asylum, and then never came back here.'

'Ha!' Etta scoffed throwing her clothes back up to the platform. 'She could have *pretended* to be hysterical, wailing about faeries and fires. She might not have expected to be put in an asylum, but she wasn't there for all that long.' Etta dropped her washcloth into the icy water on her washstand and looked up at Felix. 'I wager she planned on inheriting everything and living in luxury for the remainder of her days, but Starlings started having these awful accidents. I still believe the faeries cursed us! That put a stopper in her scheme! Maybe we're cursed *because* of her!'

Felix started scrambling down the ladder.

'But then why would Edgar have protected her? You've always said he was this wonderful big brother who helped her escape the fire and put a protection spell on her.'

Etta scrubbed at her face with the coarse flannel.

'Maybe he didn't know his sister was plotting against him? Maybe she did the protection spell on herself?' She straightened, reaching for a towel. 'We don't know enough about them! About their relationship! I've searched all the rooms of this house, read all the journals in the library, and there's no firsthand account from either of them. All we can do is go round and round with ideas, and guesses, and . . . and speculation! It's not enough!'

She threw the towel to the floor and clenched her fists.

'Something's changed since you came here, Felix. The spiders knew your name, you're hearing voices and you do something to the cobwebs. I don't know what happened in the attic, but living at Stitchwort is waking some sort of ability in you. That ability could help us find out what truly happened here all those decades ago.'

'What do you mean?' asked Felix.

'The strange voices in the bedroom, whatever that eel tornado was in the attic? Those are old, abandoned parts of the house. You've not had any problems in the kitchen or library, in our busy family areas?'

Felix slowly shook his head, thinking. 'No, nothing at all.'

'Something about the oldest cobwebs ... maybe because they've been undisturbed for so long? Spiderwebs pick up vibrations ... Maybe they stored those events, those vibrations ...'

She threw her hands in the air. 'I'm rambling, I don't know. But I think we need to go somewhere Edgar and Benita spent a lot of time and find old cobwebs, to see if ...' she shrugged. '... if you see or hear anything.'

'I did not really enjoy our time in the attic ...' Felix began tentatively.

Etta rolled her eyes. 'It won't be electric eels every time, Felix, don't be silly. Now, go and get washed and dressed. We'll have a good breakfast and pack up some supplies before we head off.'

Felix looked surprised. 'Where are we going?'

Etta beamed. 'Why, to explore the ruins, of course. Where else is there a chance of finding undisturbed old cobwebs full of clues about Edgar and Benita Starling?'

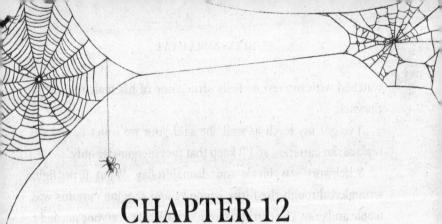

CHAPTER 12

THE MORNING WAS OVERCAST BY DARKLY luminous clouds, thick and low as wet fleece. Mother was hoping it would fall as rain, to free the grounds from the weight of the snow, but when Etta and Felix went scrambling across the icy garden to check for eggs, they were pattered with fat, slushy snowflakes that left them both damp and shivering.

Father had been busy baking straight after breakfast. He was a resourceful cook with every herb, fruit and vegetable imaginable at his fingertips. Even in these trying times there was usually something in season, and Father was a big believer in pickling, making jams and chutneys, and trying to store whatever he could.

In spite of a filling breakfast, Etta's mouth watered and her stomach grumbled as she packed herb pies, fresh, warm rolls, sticky cake, crunchy biscuits, apples and goats' cheese into her bag. Added to the rope, candles and tools she'd already packed, there was a hefty burden on her shoulder. Etta adjusted the strap of her bag and opened the door to their lantern. She watched with interest as Felix struck one of his matches and lit the wick.

'I've got my torch as well,' he said. 'But we won't be able to replace the batteries, so I'll keep that for emergencies only.'

Stitchwort was bleak and dismal today. What little light struggled through the filthy windows and sagging curtains was feeble and grey. The corridors were so dark that everyone needed a candle to avoid tripping over stray furniture, threadbare rugs and piles of books.

Etta and Felix squeezed through the gap between Etta's tree and the wall, and out into the corridor beyond. Felix gasped as Etta lifted the lantern and he saw the terrible state of this end of the house.

'What happened?' he whispered.

Down either side of the corridor were splintered doorframes where the doors had been forced open. Furniture was piled up against the windows, the darkness stifling and close. Felix shivered and rubbed his arms.

'Remember when I said my great-grandfather came here to see his ancestral family home?' Etta replied in hushed tones, as she slowly led the way. 'He and his wife had planned a sort of honeymoon, a tour of Britain, starting here at Stitchwort.'

She paused, holding the lantern up to a door that had its panels caved in. The room beyond looked thoroughly ransacked.

Etta lowered the lantern and continued. 'They're the ones who found all the letters saying that Benita Starling had fled the house after an attack by the fae and the whole family was cursed. When Cyril and his wife tried to leave Stitchwort, they were beset by near-fatal accidents and kept retreating back here to restore themselves. Eventually, they resigned themselves to the fact that they were never going to be able to make it home safely.'

'So, Cyril did all this?' Felix asked, indicating the smashed doors and covered windows.

Etta nodded. 'The house is freezing, as you've noticed.' She indicated the enormous, knitted jumper Felix wore, with an equally voluminous cardigan over it.

'And I'm still cold,' Felix muttered, linking his hands up between the rolled back sleeves.

'Oh!' Etta stopped, pulling a red woollen scarf from the bag. She wrapped it around Felix's head and neck. 'There, any better? Grandmother knitted it for me. Lovely colour, but I find it a trifle itchy. Perhaps you might get on better with it?'

Felix beamed.

'Not itchy at all, and my ears are warmer already. So, what did Cyril do?'

'Well, Grandfather just about remembers from when he was a small boy. They would go into a room, absolutely ransack it for anything useful: clothes, tools, furniture for firewood and so on. Then Cyril would board the room up to try and stop heat escaping up through the chimneys or out of the old, cracked windows.'

Felix looked back down the hall into the darkness. He couldn't make the tree out anymore, but the corridor was straight so it must have been back there somewhere.

'How did he get down here? And get furniture back out?'

Etta smiled.

'The tree wasn't as big then, this was absolutely decades ago, Felix, when my grandfather was just a boy. Since then, it's grown thicker and almost completely closed off the ruined wing of the house.' She paused, looking back in the tree's direction thoughtfully. 'I wonder if it was intentional? My tree's been very careful not to grow over the library door, or across any useful rooms. It grows away from the ruins, like it's trying to get as far away as possible. Maybe it's trying to keep us out of there?'

Felix laughed a little nervously.

They continued shuffling along, churning up the thick dust, until Etta put an arm out.

'Be careful here,' she said to Felix. 'This is the ruined bat tower.'

'Where?' asked Felix.

They were at a turn in the corridor, part of the ceiling hanging down forcing them over to their left, where a door was set diagonally in the wall. Etta looked at Felix with a quirked eyebrow and, without taking her eyes from his, she pushed at the door.

It fell away from them into the room beyond, twisting on its one remaining hinge until it hung out over empty space. If Felix had leant against it at all as he passed, he'd have fallen into the tower beyond. Swallowing, he bent his head forwards a little.

Much of the outer wall had fallen away, leaving a shard of the original tower stabbing up to the glowering sky. Clinging to the wall were the remains of the floor, just a small platform with a few supporting joists jutting out into the cavernous space like sharp fingerbones.

Peering below, Etta and Felix could see the tops of slender saplings, where the gardens were moving into the empty tower.

Another platform was above, the one Etta had made. Clustered beneath it were tiny dark shapes, huddled together.

Felix almost threw himself backwards to get away from the terrifying drop. Etta grinned cheerfully and pointed up.

'See all the bats there? What they're roosting under is my balloon workshop.' She leaned out a long way, peering up. 'I can't see the balloon at all from here.'

Felix grabbed her arm and pulled her back.

'Get away from the edge!' he snapped crossly. 'None of your spiders would come down here, so they can't rescue you if you fall out of the house.'

Etta shook him off.

'Yes, they hate it down here.' She looked around at the collapsed ceiling, sagging floor and peeling wallpaper. 'I can't think why.'

As they turned the corner, the fire damage was immediately apparent. The walls and ceiling were black, the floorboards nearly gone – only cracked, blackened joists remained in places. What little was left of the curtains hung in ragged scraps. Etta heard Felix take a deep, shaky breath behind her and carefully turned to look at him. His eyes were downcast and glassy, he was concentrating on the floor joists as he placed one foot in front of the other.

'Are you feeling well?' she asked.

Felix paused, looking around the corridor slowly.

'There are houses all over Europe that look like this now,' he said quietly, so quietly Etta strained to hear him. 'I hope my house is not like this.'

'It isn't,' Etta said firmly, giving his hand a squeeze. She moved so that they could walk side by side. 'And if it is, you can live here until we break the curse, then I'll come and help you fix it. I'm excellent at building things!'

'Etta!' Felix tugged on her hand and pointed. Ahead of them, soot-stained double doors hung open on warped hinges. Beyond, open to the sky, was a very large, completely devastated, parlour.

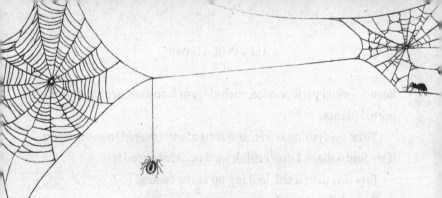

CHAPTER 13

CAUTIOUSLY THEY INCHED FORWARDS, TESTING the blackened joists and remaining floorboards with every step. A significant part of the outer wall was missing, great sheets of plaster had fallen off, exposing the brickwork. There was no glass left in the windows, just rotting frames and slimy curtains of black moss. The smell of damp and mildew was overpowering.

Felix adjusted the red scarf to cover his face, and Etta briefly regretted giving it away. Even in the bitingly cold air, she could taste the decay. Her breath puffed frozen before her, hanging there as if afraid to go any further.

They both shivered, identical tremors passing over their bodies.

'I cannot show you, under the five layers I'm wearing,' Felix whispered, moving closer to Etta. 'But I have goosebumps.'

'It feels strange,' Etta replied quietly. 'I've not been in this room before, but it's all . . . prickly and tingly. Can you hear any voices?'

Felix shook his head, looking around the room. It would have been a formal parlour once, with elegant furniture, sculptures and potted plants.

'Etta, everything is wet, and rotten, and covered in snow. Even if we find a diary, I don't think we'll be able to read it.'

Etta was distracted, looking up at the ceiling.

'Look,' she pointed.

'More cobwebs.' Felix shrugged dismissively. 'That's not unusual in Stitchwort.'

Etta shook her head firmly, her mouth set in a line. Eyes narrowed, she followed the silk strands that travelled across the room.

'This way,' she said decisively.

'Are you sure?' wondered Felix aloud, as they headed for what looked to be the worst of the decay.

Etta nodded. 'Those aren't cobwebs. Not yet anyway.'

'What do you mean?'

Etta sighed.

'Most spiders are either weavers or wanderers. Weavers make webs and wait for their prey. You'll be familiar with an orb-weaver hanging in a flat, spiral web?'

Felix nodded.

'Wanderers hunt prey down, like my wolf spiders do. There are also my jumping spiders, and my tarantulas.'

Felix grimaced. He hadn't met Etta's tarantulas yet.

'These are tangle webs,' she pointed.

'What type of spider makes them?' Felix asked, his voice a little higher than usual.

'Tangle-web spiders.' Etta tried not to laugh. 'They can hunt in packs, and they can bring down prey much bigger than themselves.'

'Like us?!' Felix froze, his hands up in a defensive position.

Etta grinned.

'No, I mean a cricket or something. They're not going to be all that big. Maybe the Stitchwort versions could take a mouse. My spiders are just oversized because of all the magic around them. This wing is all rotted and ruined – the tangle-web spiders will have left, and the magic will have too.'

She looked around, a little sadly.

'Why are we going this way then?' Felix asked.

'The tangle webs can be used to make a sort of maze, to drive prey where the pack wants it to go.' Etta pointed as she passed various lines running across the room. 'You see the trigger lines?'

Felix stopped following.

'You're leading us to where the trap wants us to go?' he asked, his eyes wide and feet stubbornly planted on the wobbly floor.

'These are old traps,' Etta insisted. 'Old traps that no longer have any spiders. But curiously haven't yet fallen apart. Tangle webs are the ones that disintegrate into cobwebs. I want to investigate, see where they go.'

'So where are these tangled webs leading?'

Etta pointed ahead to where ribbons of mildewed wallpaper formed curtains across a shadowy alcove.

There was a large painting of Stitchwort in an extremely ornate frame hanging askew in the alcove. The painting was brown with age and speckled with water marks. The canvas had swollen with damp, causing the building in the picture to bulge and the painted tower to list.

'If Mama had shown me that painting before we came here, I would have stayed in Paris,' remarked Felix as he studied it closely.

Under the filth and grime, they could see that the painting was remarkably detailed; every tiny window, every ivy leaf beautifully rendered.

Etta held the lantern close to the bottom corner and grinned savagely.

'Ha!' she said, jabbing the spongy canvas with her finger. 'Signed by Edgar Starling! I told you he was a wonderful artist. And he must have loved Stitchwort, to paint it like this! It's beautiful. Dried out and cleaned up, I bet it would be magnificent.' She straightened up. 'I've never seen any of Edgar's artwork anywhere in the house. We're getting closer to the truth!'

Felix shivered as he looked at the painting, his mouth puckered like he'd eaten something nasty.

'I don't like it, it feels wrong.' He rubbed his arms. 'This whole room feels like the attic. Can you sense it? I feel like your spiders' paws are crawling all over my skin.'

Etta nodded slowly.

'It does feel uncomfortable here, and it's not just the cold and damp.' She pointed at the web strands all around. 'It's peculiar, the way they're undisturbed in spite of this room being so radically exposed to the elements. And these,' she pointed to other threads spun through the space, 'these are the trigger lines I told you about. The tangle web funnels us here, to the painting, where we're meant to set off the trigger lines. Then what?' She looked at the nearest trigger line, finger raised.

'Please don't,' begged Felix, looking alarmed.

'There's nothing here,' Etta objected. 'I just want to see.'

'Look!' Felix said quickly. 'Hanging below the painting, it's like a cocoon! All black threads, like in the attic.' He knelt and peered closer, then jerked back.

'What?' Etta fell to her knees beside him and put her face close to the threads. 'It's like a pup tent. Some spiders make them to lay eggs in, or shed their skin, or to over-winter in. Never usually so big as this though. Did you see something inside?'

Felix leaned closer.

'I thought I heard someone speak, maybe?'

Etta's eyes widened.

'Do you think you could be hearing a memory trapped in the webs?'

Etta sat back on her heels, thinking back to all the times Felix had heard voices.

'I think you're a bit of a spider yourself,' she grinned.

'What do you mean?' Felix's voice rose in an offended pitch.

She laughed.

'I think you're sensitive to the vibrations in the silk, just like a spider is. We know spider silk soaks up magical residue from the house, that's why the spiders get so big and live so long. I can talk to spiders.' She paused. 'I think you can talk to the webs.' She pointed at the black silk pouch. 'You hear what they trap . . . Felix!' She jumped up, causing the floorboards to shriek alarmingly. 'That's IT! I knew there was something bothering me!'

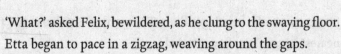

'What?' asked Felix, bewildered, as he clung to the swaying floor.

Etta began to pace in a zigzag, weaving around the gaps.

'The eels. Why on earth were there electric eels in our attic? It's been really bothering me. I know my house is a bit odd by some standards, but that really was a step too far. I've just remembered. Harold Starling!'

'Who's Harold Starling?' Felix paused. 'And if it's a long story, can I have a pie?'

Etta glared at him, then put the satchel on the floor, rather than on a mouldy, damp sofa or the charred remains of an occasional table. She threw a pie to him and took one for herself.

'Oh a fourth cousin or something[6].' Etta waved a hand airily. 'The important bit is how he died! I remember reading in the family archives that he was part of a very prestigious expedition to the Americas, exploring the Orinoco River. They drove wild horses into the river to bring the eels up out of the mud.'

'That sounds like a terrible idea,' commented Felix, spraying crumbs everywhere.

'You're right, it was an absolute fiasco. Harold lost his life in the chaos, as did many eels. And some of the poor horses.'

They were silent for a moment, thinking about the poor horses, then Etta handed Felix a slice of cheese.

'Why would Harold's ghost be here then, and not haunting the river where he died?' Felix wondered aloud.

'It must be to do with the family curse . . .' Etta said slowly. 'The curse brought all his things back here – his clothes, journals,

---

6 Actually a fifth cousin twice removed.

equipment – that's how I know about the expedition, from his research notes. He detailed the plan, that's the last entry. Maybe the curse brought Harold back too?'

'And the eels? Did the curse bring them back as well?' suggested Felix.

'Maybe. If they were all wrapped around Harold as he died, perhaps they got sort of sucked into the curse with him.' Etta's hand movements were becoming wilder as she grew more excited. 'And then ghost Harold and the ghost eels got caught by the spiderwebs in the attic!'

Felix burst out laughing.

'Spiderwebs catch flies Etta, not ghosts!'

'In a house that's been owned by generations of witches, a house steeped in magic? We know the spider silk absorbs surplus magical energy. Have you ever noticed how a spiderweb doesn't just hang there passively? It moves towards the prey as they fly by. They have an energy within them.' She dusted the crumbs off her hands and stood up, hands on hips as she glared at the knot of silk hanging beneath the painting.

'Whatever the scientific reason, I think our spiderwebs can catch more than just flies.' She pointed at the silk pocket. 'I think you're hearing what else they've trapped in those webs. I think the cobwebs around Elizabeth Starling's bed held her memories, or her dreams maybe, but the ones in the attic held Harold Starling's ghost.'

'And we squashed him and those eels together and threw him across the attic!' exclaimed Felix, horrified. 'He said "Help me"!'

'We can help Harold later.' Etta stepped closer to the snarl of silk. 'You heard a voice here. Do you think it could be a memory, or another ghost?'

'Let's not find out,' suggested Felix.

Etta looked at him, her eyes wide.

'Felix! They could have been trapped in there for over a century! They might have information about the curse! We might find answers! We might find . . .' She raised her clenched fists to her jaw and did a little shuffle of excitement. '. . . Edgar Starling!' she squealed.

Felix looked doubtfully at the tangled threads of the black cocoon.

'What if there are more eels?'

'There won't be. Harold was the only one killed by eels. And he probably died of drowning after the eels knocked him out.'

'Comforting,' said Felix, following a strand of silk with his fingers.

'Although Thomas Starling was killed when he got in between a mother bear and her cub,' Etta recalled. 'The bears were fine though, so I doubt we'd get a ghost bearcub.' She rummaged in her bag for the biscuits. 'Sadly.'

Felix tugged gently at the strand and shivered. Etta looked up as a tingling wave washed over her body.

'Did you feel that too?' she asked.

Felix nodded, loosening another line of thread with a soft tug.

'This is just like Mama's sewing box,' he complained.

Etta sat back, munching on her biscuit as Felix methodically loosened the strands, freeing the cocoon from below the painting. The waves of goosebumps and tingles began to irritate her, so she moved a little further away, peering around the ruined room. Against the dullness of the day another trigger line shone bright silver in the air before her.

Checking over her shoulder, Etta gently tapped it, watching as ripples danced slowly along the line, increasing their speed and frequency as they approached the wall. Etta followed the vibrations, observing as they travelled to one of the darkest corners of the room . . .

Where something in the shadows shifted.

CHAPTER 14

ETTA STEPPED BACK THEN, CLOSER TO FELIX, the back of her neck prickling with danger.

'Felix?' she whispered, flinching at how loud her whisper seemed now. Before, the room had been dormant, but now it felt alert, and listening.

The vibrations continued to hum across the parlour, the filaments of silk leaping. All around the room were dark patches; places where the black mould spread across the walls like pawprints and the harsh charcoal burn marks blended into the moth-soft shadows.

Now, each dark place twitched with surreptitious movement, stirring slightly. Etta knew something was there – she could sense it, feel it. But she couldn't see anything.

Scanning the walls again, Etta felt anxiety squirm in her guts as thin, smooth legs began unfolding, very, very slowly, from a sizeable crack in the plaster.

She concentrated, feeling for a connection with the spider. Normally, it felt like trying to make out the words of a conversation in another room, but she could hear nothing except light pattering as little chunks of mortar rained onto the floorboards. After the first two long legs came a flash of green iridescence, before the spider's feelers began to tap and touch the edges of the crack.

Green fangs?

Etta took another step back, so that she was right next to Felix. He was knelt, facing away from her, the tangled ball of silk now three times the size as he gently teased the strands apart.

'Felix, I don't wish to worry you,' she muttered out of the corner of her mouth. As she did so, the fabric of a sofa cushion on the other side of the room distended outwards. Straining her eyes to see in the dim light, Etta saw the faded stripes stretch further and further to a peak, then another hard, shiny black leg tore through with a shockingly loud ripping sound.

The leg slowly unfurled as the rotten material peeled away. As the sodden stuffing bulged out of the rips, the remains of a pigeon slid wetly out, scattering tatty feathers.

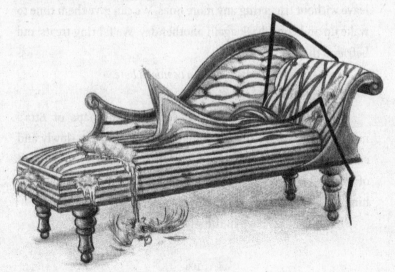

'They're just spiders, Felix,' Etta reasoned. 'I know you don't really like spiders, but they won't hurt you. They've probably been in here, dormant, for decades. It's very cold and some species do hibernate. We've just woken them up, that's all.'

They are rather larger than I had expected, though, thought Etta. *And I have the awful feeling they might have woken up a little grumpy.*

Counting the other stirrings in the room, there were at least three of them.

Of course, black widows are a type of tangle-web spider . . .

If she and Felix headed for the door now, they might make it. Again, Etta tried to reach out to the spiders, to explain that they were friends. But it was like running into a wall of cold metal – her mind slid off, and there was a painful little pinch behind her forehead. Like a little stinging slap warning her not to try again.

'Etta?' Felix's voice was shaky. 'What were you just saying? Do you . . . do you think we should leave now? Etta?'

'It's alright, Felix,' she reassured him. 'We just need to carefully leave without triggering any more lines. We can give them time to wake up and come back again another day. We'll bring treats and befriend them.'

Now I know why my spiders won't come in here.

'But what about . . . her?' asked Felix.

An icy trickling sensation flowed from the nape of Etta's neck all the way to her toes. With great restraint, she slowly and carefully turned around to see Felix still kneeling, his fingers full of dusty silk threads. More spider silk pooled on the floor around him, from where he'd painstakingly loosened the mess of webs.

Standing ankle deep in the silk stood a girl.

She looked to be about their age and wore a simple pale shift. Her long hair was loose and clung to her, like it was damp. Her eyes were unusual, very large and dark, with hardly any white showing.

The girl stared at the ruined parlour behind them, her eyes flitting from the collapsed wall to the holey floor. She shrank back into the corner of the alcove. Actually *into* the wall, Etta realised. The girl's shoulder had disappeared into a curl of wet wallpaper.

Etta squinted at the pale shift; she could make out the mould growing up the wall behind right through the girl's dress.

'She's a ghost!' Etta blurted, a penetrating cold wrapping tight around her skin. 'A real ghost, trapped in the cobwebs!'

Felix was rigid, staring at the ghost. He reached out a cold hand and squeezed Etta's fingers until she felt her bones grate.

'You're surprised that you were right?' he hissed.

'Well, I just . . . I didn't expect us to find one so quickly.'

'What should we do?'

'Slowly step back, she hasn't seen us yet. And stop breaking my hand.'

Etta didn't know how the ghost hadn't noticed them; they were standing almost right in front of her. The girl's brow furrowed as she looked at her hands, turning them back and forth. She was a pale sort of silvery grey, and dappled, like the surface of the moon on a clear night.

She held her hands up and stared at them, stared *through* them. She was looking at the ivy growing from the ceiling through her own skin. Her face started to crumple, as though she was going to cry.

She didn't know, Etta realised, horrified.

'Etta,' Felix murmured close to her ear. 'Etta, I don't think she . . .'

They both stopped backing away from the ghost, her desolate expression halting their retreat.

Etta slowly let out a breath she hadn't realised she was holding. She checked behind them for the spiders, which were still slowly extracting themselves from their hiding places. They had a little time, she hoped.

Etta crossed her fingers and stepped forward.

'Hello,' she said tentatively to the ghost, remembering at the last minute to put on a smile. She added a wave, to try and get the girl's attention.

The ghost's eyes focused on Etta, and a delighted smile of recognition broke across her face. Etta felt the faintest of voices brush against her mind.

Benita

The ghost tried to run forwards, her arms out, but one foot was still ensnared in the webbing.

Felix flinched away as one of her arms passed through his.

'Ugh, that's horrible.' He shuddered. 'Like gutter water falling down inside your collar.'

The girl's smile fell as she looked more closely at Etta. She searched Etta's face, then looked away sadly. Etta came and stood in front of her.

'I'm Henrietta Starling,' she said, holding out her hand as Father had taught her, hoping the ghost didn't notice the tremor in her voice. 'I suppose we can't really shake hands, can we?' She gave an embarrassed smile.

The ghost's movements were slow and languid, like she was hearing them from underwater.

Starling?

The question flowed through Etta's mind like an incoming wave. Etta's neck crawled from the feel of it, cold and slick as sea glass, but she tried to hide her reaction and be polite.

'Yes, I'm Etta Starling, and this is Felix. He's trying to free you.' She waved a hand at Felix to get on with it while Etta had her distracted. 'You were trapped in a cobweb, I think. What's your name?'

Felix quickly crouched behind the ghost. Keeping her in sight, he worked faster than ever on the binding threads.

The ghost considered Etta for a moment. Her eyes were fathoms deep, black and endless. When she looked at Etta it felt like being swallowed up in a dark cave.

Marin

The word fell into Etta's mind, sending ripples across her brain. Etta shook her head to shake the feeling, not at all enjoying how the ghost communicated.

'It's nice to meet you, Marin,' Etta replied. Now that they'd met a ghost, what were they supposed to do with it? She didn't recognise the name Marin from any of the family records.

Marin was looking around the room, at the gaping roof, the collapsed wall, the huge holes in the floor. She pointed to the missing wall.

What?

'This must have happened after you . . .' Etta paused, thinking an attempt at tact might be wise, '. . . er, after you lived here. There was a fire, it destroyed most of the west wing.'

There was no fire.

Etta and Felix exchanged a glance. There was another long pause, like waiting for the next wave to wash in. Then:

I did not live here

I died here

'Who is she?' hissed Felix. 'What's she doing here?' He gave a final jiggle of the strands and the last of the web fell away from Marin's ankle. She quickly pulled her foot free, careful to make sure she didn't touch the spiderwebs again.

Felix scuttled around Marin and grasped Etta, digging his nails into her arm. It hurt, even through both her jumpers.

'She's floating,' he gasped under his breath.

After Marin had pulled her foot free, she'd continued to bob up slightly and now hovered before them, her head higher than theirs.

Where is it?

Please?

'Where is what?' Etta asked, her nose scrunched up.

Return it

Etta and Felix exchanged a bewildered glance.

'Return what?' Etta asked.

The rest of me

'Felix, did you leave a bit of her behind?' Etta cried, aghast, as she stared at the unravelled heap of web.

'No!' Felix sounded outraged. 'I was very careful!'

No not again

Marin's voice dropped, hollow and loud. It cracked across their minds like breaking ice.

Etta and Felix clutched at each other, braced for the ghost to swoop down upon them in vengeful wrath.

But Marin was looking past them, at something that frightened her so much her face twisted in terror and she held her arms up in defence.

'Etta!' gasped Felix, pointing to a large, black spider edging across the ceiling towards them.

Etta moved in front of Felix.

'Felix, Marin, go towards the door,' she ordered, stepping to the right and trying to keep between them and the spider.

'What kind of spider is it?' Felix whispered from behind her. 'Is it poisonous?'

'Were you planning on eating it?' grumbled Etta. 'Or did you mean venomous?'

'You know what I mean!' She could hear the scowl in Felix's voice.

'Well, I'm not sure exactly.' Etta had been assessing the spider ever since she'd first laid eyes on it. 'Long body, comb-footed, smooth, shiny exoskeleton, almost scorpion-like.' She paused. 'Those green jaws look powerful, try not to let them grab you with those.'

'*Them?* There are more?' Felix moaned in dread, as he came so close he stepped on Etta's heels.

'They're working together in a pack.' Etta pursed up her lips as she assessed the spiders' characteristics. 'I think they made the tangle webs.'

As she backed them away from it, Etta really hoped Felix wouldn't notice that the spider on the ceiling had a sheet web stretched taut between its legs, ready to drop onto them if they came within range. She quickly glanced to see what Marin was doing – could the ghost help them?

Marin was near the centre of the room, floating midway between the remnants of the floor and the gaping roof. She moved like a ripple in a stream, weaving slowly through the webs like a fish. She was hesitant, careful not to make a wrong move or get too close as she examined the destruction.

Etta could feel the ghost's agitation, and her confusion, it thrummed along her nerves.

Not real

'What isn't real?' They were just edging past the fireplace, where a poker and tongs lay on the cracked grate. Etta reached for them, silently passing the tongs to Felix.

Marin turned gently, her arm gesture encompassing the whole room.

'Clear as mud,' complained Felix under his breath.

'The spiders aren't real?' Etta asked. She and Felix exchanged a glance, then looked at the spiders. The one on the ceiling was having to go the long way around, because of the holes in the roof. The one still exiting the sofa was extracting its last leg, and another one was softly but relentlessly scratching at the plaster to free itself from the wall.

'Have I lost one?' Etta whispered.

'I think we should continue as if they *are* real,' muttered Felix, hefting the tongs and giving them a practise swing.

'Agreed,' said Etta, gritting her teeth and continuing to creep past the fireplace.

Spiders bad

'Yes Marin, thank you,' said Etta absently, planning their route across the floor to avoid both the spiders and any boards that wouldn't take their weight.

Took the rest of me

'What does that mean?' wondered Felix. 'How can they take away a part of you?'

'Oh no . . .' Etta realised. She quickly scanned the room. 'If the spiders attacked her, if they . . .' She didn't want to say the words where Marin could hear. 'Think about it, Felix. What do spiders do with prey? What happens when they catch a fly?'

Felix's eyes bulged at Etta in horror.

'You think she's looking for her . . . I mean, I suppose that would be the "rest of her".' His voice dropped low and quiet. 'You mean her . . . *remains*,' he hissed. 'They're in this room?' He shuddered, his mouth twisted down in a grimace as his gaze crawled miserably around the dark lumps and shadows of the destroyed room.

Etta's flesh crawled, thinking of the husks of mice, rats and bats she sometimes came across in quiet corners of the house.

'We're leaving. Now,' she announced determinedly, taking a firm step towards the exit.

Behind her, Felix cried out and sprawled forwards, a spider's legs wrapped around his face.

CHAPTER 15

ETTA SCREAMED, BRANDISHING THE POKER AS she turned to see a tangle-web spider had ambushed Felix from the empty fireplace behind them. It had pounced onto Felix's back, knocking him to the ground while trying to clench its powerful jaws around his neck. Luckily, the scarf, jumper and cardigan Felix was wearing were protecting him, but his woollen defenses were rapidly unravelling.

One pair of the spider's legs held on to the grate, already hauling Felix back to the chimney. The rest were scrabbling at the struggling prey, trying to incapacitate him with an envenomating bite.

I'm so stupid! Etta thought, furious with herself for only now seeing the silk threads radiating out from the fireplace. *It's got some sort of tube web up the chimney!* Etta gripped her poker firmly and swung it at the creature's head, narrowly missing Felix's ear.

The blow landed and, caught off guard, the spider toppled off Felix, landing on its back, legs thrashing the air. Etta's hand and wrist ached from the shock of the blow. On the ceiling, Marin began wailing; an awful, icy keening that made Etta's head feel like it was packed with snow.

Before the spider could turn over, Etta swung the poker again, aiming for its soft, exposed abdomen. There was an awful noise, like dropping a soaking wet towel onto a stone floor, then a terrible, sickly sour smell as the poker broke the glossy exoskeleton and sank into the spider's soft middle. It began to twitch and shake even more violently, drumming the floor with its knees.

With a hideous drawn-out groaning, the floor collapsed beneath it and the jerking spider disappeared into the darkened room below.

Etta and Felix looked at each other from opposite sides of the hole.

'Are you hurt?' Etta asked Felix quickly. She couldn't tell if the spider had bitten him, his neck was so wound round with the red scarf. A wave of nausea passed over Etta, and for a moment she couldn't bear to look at the scarlet gash of wool at his throat.

Felix carefully felt his head, checking his ears and nose were still there.

'I think I'm alright. You?'

Etta carefully took a step. The floor was even less secure now. She quickly scanned the room.

'Where are they all?'

'The tangles?' Felix asked. 'The ceiling one is over there, the one that came from the wall is behind that chair and the one from the sofa climbed up the wall when the floor collapsed. It's under that curl of paper.'

'Tangles?' asked Etta.

'Tangle-web spiders. Tangles is easier.' Felix flashed a forced grin.

'Tangles it is,' Etta agreed grimly. 'We need to get Marin and get out of here. I hate to admit it, but my parents might be right. The ruins are perilous.'

Felix had started edging around the new hole in the floor.

'Do we have to bring her?' he asked, shooting a grim look at the wailing ghost. He was moving very cautiously, like a mountain climber; one foot, then one hand, then the other foot, then the other hand.

'She knows something.' Etta watched the ghost rocking herself on the ceiling, her arms wrapped tightly around herself. 'I think she was here, before . . .'

'I think she's shell-shocked,' said Felix, as he reached the fireplace.

Etta didn't know what that meant, but the 'shocked' part sounded right. The ghost looked thoroughly panic-stricken.

'She did just find out she's dead,' agreed Etta. 'That's got to be quite the adjustment.'

Felix made a small jump from the fireplace to Etta's side.

'Please say we're leaving immediately,' he pressed. He looked up at the ghost. 'What do you think she knows?'

'She thought I was Benita Starling when she first saw me – she smiled at me. I think they were friends maybe? She might know about Edgar and his sister.' Etta spotted her satchel of supplies on the far side of the room.

'Botheration,' she grumbled. 'Our food and equipment.'

'My torch!' moaned Felix.

Etta linked arms with Felix, giving him an apologetic squeeze.

'When Marin saw the tangles she said, "not again". She's seen them before. She avoided the trigger lines as well as the spiders. She knows something about what happened here. We must question her.' Etta looked towards her. 'Marin? Marin, we're going now. Come over here,' Etta called.

Marin turned in the air to face them, then looped and twisted her way through the filaments of silk, carefully avoiding becoming trapped again.

Just as the ghost reached them there was a long groan from the floor, a creak which rose into a whine, and the part Etta and Felix were standing on gave way, pitching them into the room below.

The heap they landed in was spongey, slimy and cold. Etta rolled onto her side, feeling her back and ribs ache.

'Yuck,' she grumbled, recoiling from the assorted revolting textures. 'I think it's a good thing it's too dark to see what this is.'

'Ugh,' Felix groaned, propping up on his elbows. Then 'Aaaargh!' as he saw the face of the fireplace spider between his ankles. He kicked out instinctively and pushed it off the heap.

The room they had fallen into was black and burnt as well. The floor from above had collapsed into this room, creating a haphazard jumble of furniture, broken ornaments and floorboards. Luckily, there was a large billiards table in the centre, which had broken their fall a little. An empty bookcase loomed drunkenly over them, the sodden books were piled on the baize table surface, slowly rotting into slimy pulp.

It was even darker down here, the trees were growing in

through the damaged walls and windows, blocking out the light. Brambles looped everywhere.

Marin swooped down and stared at them. Etta noticed she had a faint luminescent glow.

Hurt?

'I don't think so,' Etta reassured her.

'Can we get out from down here?' asked Felix, sitting up carefully.

Etta nodded, wobbling as she stood, assessing the thick brambles that were overgrowing everything from her vantage point on the table.

'We could really use Mother ordering that lot back.'

Felix slid down the heap of decaying books onto the floor, landing crouched and catlike. He stood, pointing.

'Can we get to that branch? We could walk along it to the trunk outside. Hopefully then there'll be a clear path to the ground.'

Etta smiled up at the glowing ghost. 'Are you ready to come outside, Marin?'

Marin gave the smallest of smiles, looking hopefully out of the windows, then gave a joyous loop the loop above Etta. Etta laughed softly with her as she readied to jump down.

The tangle-web spider from the ceiling above dropped down on to them, its sheet web stretched out wide between its long legs.

Marin and Etta were caught as one, both pinned beneath the net. The ghost girl stuck fast to the silk strands as they fell around Etta, pushing her through Etta's body. Felix was yelling something far away, but Marin's screams were shards of ice cutting through Etta's temples, the psychic assault halting all sound and reason.

The tangle started to tuck and gather the net around them, curving its abdomen to spin dark silk from its spinnerets, weaving and combing the strands with its hind legs.

Etta was momentarily stunned, but as she felt the net tighten around her, felt the spider's paws jostle her, she knew they had to move urgently.

She tried to block out Marin's screaming and ignore the sensation of the ghost's limbs passing through her own as Marin thrashed within her. The spider's mouthparts were chittering above her, the fangs visible beneath the green iridescence.

Etta concentrated. Taking a deep breath, she felt for a connection. *Stop!* she commanded the spider. *Let us go.*

If the tangle heard her, it paid her no heed and continued to tighten the net around them. Marin's wailing within Etta began to burn like frostbite and she felt her temper rise.

Etta gathered herself again and glared through the binding net into the spider's black eyes. She thrust her will towards the spider, using her anger to try to force a connection, to compel it to submit to her.

The spider staggered to the side, its knees buckling. The screaming stopped.

The pause gave Etta a chance to sit up as Felix came scrambling back up the mound of books and together they tore the net off, throwing it, and Marin, to the floor. As Etta rose to a crouch, she knelt on the poker she'd been holding when they'd fallen through the floor.

'Help Marin,' Etta said, as she pushed Felix down the pile of books away from the tangle. The spider was shaking off her mental attack, it raised the front of its body threateningly, front legs splayed wide in the air and fangs flaring. Etta whirled the poker and thrust it at the spider, again and again like a fencer, driving it back. The mound of rubbish they were standing on began to shift from the ferocity of their battle, books and indistinct items shook loose and began to slide past the spider as it backed away from her savage onslaught. Glass and pots shattered all around as they reached the floor.

Etta had the high ground, the charred bookcase leaning crookedly to her left. The spider darted forwards but staggered as one of its feet slipped into a billiards pocket.

Seeing her chance, Etta pulled hard, dragging the bookcase over between her and the trapped spider.

'Felix!' she called, ducking as a long leg scratched at the air above her. Felix came scrambling back up the mound, a curved sliver of broken glass in one hand and a ragged section of the tangles net in the other. Together they heaved against the bookcase, using it as a shield to push the tangle down onto the floor.

Etta grabbed a handful of net from Felix and they stretched it taut between them. She took a swift glance around the end of the bookcase, to check the spider's position. It was still sorting its legs out and seemed a little stunned.

'Now,' she said to Felix, and they rushed it, stretching the net to take in the spider's head, feelers and front legs. Before it could even react, they'd met around the back, where they quickly pulled the threads tight, like a drawstring bag. The spider hissed and clicked, the bundle thrashing on the floor amongst glittering pieces of broken glass.

'Will that hold it?' Felix asked quietly. He was crouched near, his fingers trembling.

Etta nodded, feeling a little queasy.

She stiffly stood from the bookcase, new aches and bruises clamouring for her attention. 'Where's Marin?'

Felix reached for Marin, who was quiet and still now. She was curled into a ball beneath the rest of the spiderweb net, her arms wrapped around her knees. He held out a shard of broken pottery to Etta.

'After you've cut through the net you have to peel it off her. It's not sticky for us but snags on her somehow,' he whispered.

They worked in silence, cutting and removing the rest of the web until the silent, shaking Marin was free. As they bundled the web up and away from her, the ghost shot into the air and flew out through the charred window frame.

'Marin!' called Etta. 'Wait!' She turned and helped Felix to his feet. 'We have to go after her, we must help her. She's terrified.'

'Give me a minute,' Felix insisted, leaning forward with his hands on his knees, taking a few shaky breaths. 'That was awful.'

Etta looked up towards the hole that took up most of the ceiling.

'It was. But I think we should definitely get out of here quickly. We don't know if there's any more tangles coming.'

Felix took a gulp of air and backed towards the outer wall, keeping his eyes firmly fixed on the ceiling.

The fallen bricks and rubble fell away as they muddled their way out over a disintegrating window ledge and dropped down onto the snowy ground outside.

Etta looked back up at her home, feeling deeply sad to see part of the beautiful house in such a state. There was no denying how creepy the decaying wing was, even more so now that she knew about the hostile tangleweb spiders.

Whole walls were missing, she could look right into not just the rooms themselves, but at what lay between the rooms – the secret cavities between one floor and another, one wall and the next, seeing the very bones of Stitchwort.

Etta took a step back, certain there were not-quite-human faces watching from the shadows. She shook herself, there was no time for fancies now. They'd freed the ghost, and now they had to rescue her.

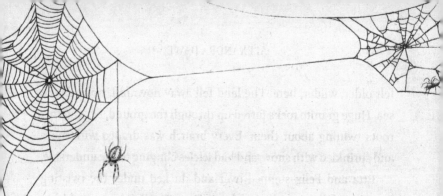

CHAPTER 16

STITCHWORT WAS CLOSE TO THE WOODS HERE. They were almost immediately under the cover of the trees, the boughs weighed down by the thick snow.

It was bone-bitingly cold. The afternoon was as dull as the morning had been, the weak light barely penetrating the frosted gloom between the contorted trunks. Sound was muffled, like they had tepid bathwater in their ears.

Etta's breath puffed in little clouds in front of her, and Felix wheezed from the cold in his chest. Their feet crunched on the frozen ground which didn't give way at all, the forest floor hard as bricks.

Somewhere under the trees, Marin began singing. The sound penetrated their temples like needles of frost.

'This way,' said Etta, stepping down a faint holloway formed by wildlife. 'We can follow her singing. It's louder this way?' She checked if Felix agreed. He was dishevelled and dusty, with numerous cuts and grazes, but he gave a firm nod.

They made their way through the dense thicket. The woods

felt older, wilder, here. The land fell away downhill, towards the sea. Huge granite rocks jutted up through the ground, ivy and tree roots twining about them. Every branch was draped with moss and sprinkled with snow, and had icicles clinging to the underside.

Etta and Felix stepped over and ducked under the twisting branches, following the lonely singing. Finally, they saw Marin floating in the air ahead of them, scratching at her skin.

'Marin!' Etta called. 'The spider's gone, it's alright. We can help you!'

The ghost broke off her song, her face anguished, then drifted back and disappeared inside a pile of snow-dusted granite stones below a gnarled oak tree.

'Can we help her?' Felix asked, as they ran forwards. 'How are we going to help her?'

They reached the stand of boulders and quickly circled them.

'Where'd she go?' asked Felix. 'Why didn't she come out the other side?'

Etta frowned up at the grey rocks which had thick, mossy tree roots twining around them. She traced her fingers over some marks in the stone.

'I think she came here deliberately. Her first flight into the woods might have been blind panic, but that song . . . I think she recognised where she was and deliberately came here.'

'But you don't think she's a Starling?' Felix asked, rubbing his frozen hands together.

Etta shook her head, slowly walking around the rocky outcrop. 'There's no mention of a Marin in our family records, but she was convinced she died here. It's about the only thing she did seem

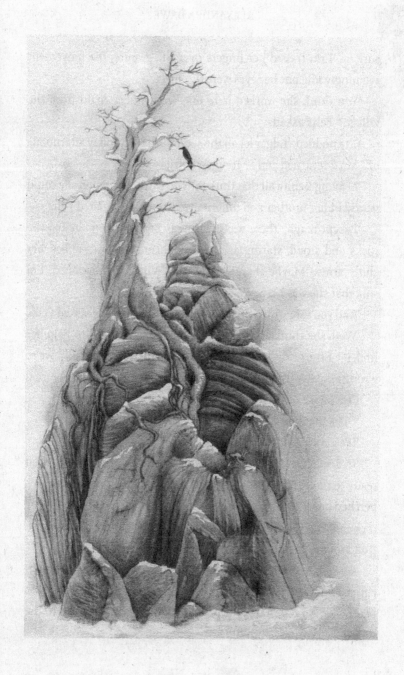

sure of.' Etta trailed her fingers over the granite, the movement seemingly idle but her eyes were intent.

'You think she worked here maybe? A house maid from the village?' Felix asked.

Etta nodded. 'Edgar let all the servants have Sunday afternoons off. Most returned early Monday mornings.'

'Leaving Benita all that time with no witnesses, when she could get rid of her brother and inherit everything,' speculated Felix.

'Except maybe there *was* a witness.' Etta stopped circling the rocks and stood, staring at one thoughtfully as she rubbed her chilly arms. 'Maybe there was Marin. Whatever happened, I'm sure that she was here. We have to question her.'

'And you said we'd help her – but help her do what?' asked Felix.

'Well, she thinks she's lost something, so we need to help her find it.' Etta grimaced. 'Whatever it might be. Hopefully we're wrong about . . . that!'

Etta paused, still frowning at one particular boulder.

'Does that one strike you as odd?' she asked Felix.

'It's a rock, same as all the others.'

'It doesn't seem sort of . . .' Etta paused, her finger poised ready to poke the offending stone, '. . . gravity defying, the way it's perched here?' She gently nudged it and grinned delightedly as the rock moved. 'Ha!' she crowed triumphantly. 'It's a counterweight. Run around the other side and tell me if a doorway appears.'

At Felix's excited shouting, Etta followed to see a rough-cut rectangular passage, with uneven steps leading down into blackness. An old, fraying rope had been roughly fastened to the walls to serve as a handrail.

'Listen!' Felix held up a finger. They both stilled, tilting their heads.

'What did you hear?' Etta whispered.

They both heard it then, not a quiet noise but a loud one, far away. A dull roar boomed for a few seconds, then faded.

'What on earth was that?' Etta asked, her eyes enormous.

Felix grinned. 'That was the sea!'

A second later, Marin's voice slipped into Etta's mind, cold as a pebble.

Where is it?

She saw Felix flinch and knew he'd heard it too. They looked up to see the ghost floating half out of the rocks above them.

'I don't know, but we'll help you,' Etta reassured her.

'Whatever it is,' added Felix darkly. 'It might take a while though; it's a very messy house.'

The sea boomed again, and Marin's liquid black eyes flicked from them to the opening. Darting like a fish, she slipped inside.

'Wait!' cried Etta, grabbing for her. 'We don't know what's down there!'

Etta and Felix stood at the threshold. Set into the wall above the rotting handrail were shells and ammonites. Etta ran her fingers across their cool forms.

'We've found a secret passage!' She grinned.

Felix looked less impressed. 'It's dark as night down there.'

'And we left the satchel behind,' Etta grumbled. 'All our supplies and equipment.' She went a few steps in.

'Wait, do you have a light?' Felix quickly asked, coming after her. 'We lost the torch.'

Too quickly, the hidden door thunked shut behind them, plunging them into blackness. Felix gasped.

Etta was smiling, her hair glowing like lavender smoke. 'It's never dark when you're with me, Felix.'

'How is your hair glowing?' asked Felix, watching Etta's thick mass of luminous lilac curls bob along in front of him.

'It isn't really, it's the spiderlings that glow. I don't like the bigger spiders staying in my hair all day, they tickle and itch, but I don't notice the little babies at all.'

She said this as though it was perfectly normal to have spiders living in your hair. Felix stared at the back of her head silently for a moment, then decided it was best not to comment.

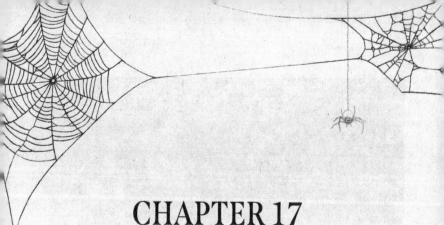

CHAPTER 17

AS THE STEPS GREW STEEPER, THEY STOPPED talking to better concentrate. The echoes of their footsteps were the only sound.

Tired

'Marin?' Felix called. He looked at Etta, puzzled.

'Marin!' Etta cried as they came upon her. The ghost bobbed listlessly along the corridor, as though she had no energy. Etta knew how she felt – her knees were aching, her limbs heavy and her extremities numb with cold. Her little spiderlings were tiring and giving them less light.

'What's wrong with her?' asked Felix.

'How would I know?' Etta retorted irritably. 'I'm not an expert on ghosts. Maybe she needs to rest, or maybe she's too far from,' she dropped her voice to a low mutter, 'you know, her remains?'

The sea roared louder, and they started to feel a breeze. The walls ran with moisture and the ceiling dripped on them. Marin brightened a little at the breeze and swayed slightly in the corridor, as though she could hear music.

'I think it's lighter ahead,' called Felix as he ran past the ghost, pointing to where the steps curved around.

'I don't know how far we've come, or where we are,' Etta said. 'We've twisted and turned so many times I could believe we're under our house, or even the village!' She paused doubtfully. 'Felix? Do you think this tunnel is technically still part of Stitchwort?'

She hurried to catch him up, to ask again, but was distracted as she rounded the bend.

'Felix, this is . . .' Etta was lost for words, her exhaustion vanishing at the sight before her.

The narrow passage opened on to a shelf of grey rock, high in the walls of a large cave. Below them, enormous slabs of granite stepped down to a wide strip of sand, dotted with rocks, pools and channels. Waves swelled and rolled in to break on the shore with a booming crash that echoed around the cave. The roof arched above then down to the incoming sea, like a mouth closing on the waves.

'Rock pools!' Etta cried joyously. She immediately jumped down to the next rock, ready to descend to the beach in the fastest way possible.

'Etta!' called Felix, pointing to the side of the passage doorway.

There were a few tins, rags and assorted equipment, all piled on top of a small crate beside the opening. Past this was another rope handrail and a path of rope bridges leading between the rocks.

'This might be quicker.'

Etta smirked impishly. 'Race you!' she challenged and carried on scrambling down the tiered rocks to the beach. Behind her she heard Felix laughing and looked over her shoulder to see him running across the first bridge.

The race was already forgotten when Etta jumped off the last rock on to the damp sand and ran towards Felix, shrieking and laughing, tasting salt on her lips from the spray in the air.

'I've always wanted to go to the beach and see a rock pool! This is the best day I've ever had!'

She clambered up a heap of rocks, crawling to put her face close to the pools.

'They're incredible, all these tiny worlds! I love them!'

'Look over there,' called Felix, pointing across the beach. Etta stood, then, cheering and whooping, they both ran across the sand.

On the other side of the cave was a ship, listing over with the stern partially submerged. The bow lay on the beach, crumpled over the rocks with its deck collapsed inwards. Exotic-looking plants sprouted from the inside and trailed across the wreck. Along that side of the cave the remains of a dock were sinking under the surging sea. The remnants of old rowboats were pulled up high on the beach, their desiccated remains fastened to iron hooks driven into the rock. On the very highest rocks were crates, lanterns, coiled ropes and all manner of nautical gear.

'The tide must go a long way out to have let that ship in!' Felix shouted. He was delighted by the cave, his eyes sparkled, and a wide grin threatened to split his face in two.

Etta assessed the ship, her head on one side.

'The masts are snapped,' she called to Felix over the booming of the sea. 'Do you think it tried to come in when the tide was too high for it to fit under the cave entrance?'

'Maybe there was a storm that threw it against the rocks?' Felix hopped from rock to rock to keep his feet dry. The little sand beach was rapidly vanishing under the incoming tide.

'Or maybe,' suggested Etta thoughtfully, 'Stitchwort used to use this as a private mooring . . . All those family scientists going on expeditions, bringing back samples and artefacts. Maybe the curse wrecked someone's boat as they were returning home.'

Etta looked at all the crates and equipment sadly.

'I suppose all those plants were supposed to be in our collection, but they were lost down here when the ship was wrecked.'

She felt a pang, imagining how in a different life she would have skipped down here to join her parents on a voyage, or one day captain a ship herself.

Maybe it could still happen? Felix could be my first mate? she considered.

'I'm going to have a look!' shouted Felix, throwing his arms in the air as he ran.

Etta followed, but slowly as she examined every new thing; the texture of the sand, the mussel shells clinging to the rocks, everything was new and bright to her excited eyes and exploring fingers. As she looked up at the imposing wreck, a tiny niggle of doubt started gnawing at her brain.

'Felix?' she called, as she watched the waves lurching into the cavern one after the other, relentlessly. 'Felix, do you think we're safe from the curse in here?'

The waves were too loud to hear if he'd replied or not, so with a last, longing look at the ship, Etta followed him up the rocks.

Felix had climbed higher than Etta expected, exploring the labyrinth of planks, rope ladders and walkways that criss-crossed the rocks and ledges. He'd found an ancient, three-cornered hat when she reached him, the leather cracked and salt-stained.

'What is all this?' asked Etta.

'It's definitely not just washed here,' Felix said, cramming the hat down over his hair. 'I think you're right; our ancestors had their own little port here.' His eyes widened. 'Ooooh, do you think they were smugglers and pirates?' he asked, his voice lowered in a conspiratorial whisper.

'Absolutely not.' Etta was outraged at the very idea. 'They would never steal or smuggle! Our ancestors were very honourable.'

Felix looked quite disgruntled by this and turned his attention to a pile of crates instead.

'Do you think we're still under the Stitchwort grounds?' Etta asked. 'Or do you think this beach would count as part of it, if it's our mooring?'

'I don't know,' Felix replied, trying to prise open a crate with his bare hands. 'Why do you ask?'

'The curse,' Etta replied. 'Fun though this is, we shouldn't linger here in case we're not safe. There's nothing here that can help us answer our questions, and we've lost Marin again.'

Felix nodded slowly, seeming reluctant to give up on opening the box.

'Felix, I'll bring my crowbar down for you next time,' Etta promised. 'Please, let's find Marin and come back properly prepared.'

Felix muttered something sulkily under his breath, then hopped down to the next rock.

'Etta?' he said shakily. 'Etta, look.'

She looked down over the edge of the shelf at the churning, swirling waves that were coming up to meet them.

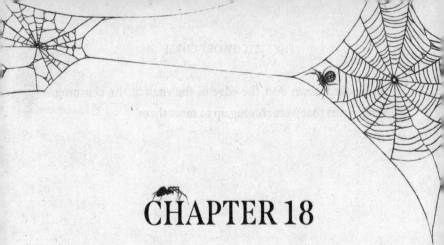

CHAPTER 18

FELIX SCRAMBLED BACK UP TO ETTA.

'The tide's coming in so fast!'

He pointed at the way the cavern roof sloped down to make a curved opening for the sea. Already it was more like a sleepily closed eye than a gaping mouth.

'The opening disappears completely under the sea!' Felix squeaked.

Etta looked around, noticing how little light remained in the cave. She tried to speak nonchalantly so as not to frighten Felix. Being brave helped to squash the rising panic that squeezed her lungs.

'You can see from the tideline the water doesn't reach up to where we came in. We'll have plenty of time to make our way back to the passage without even getting our feet wet.'

They carefully began to make their way across the shelves and ledges, helping each other across. Some of their ancestors' bridges had disintegrated; they had to climb lower in search of another way. All the while the water level rose, far too fast to be natural,

Etta thought. Their ears ached from the endless din of it, booming and echoing around the cave.

There came a moment when they both realised the last of the light was about to be lost. Etta strained her eyes trying to work out how far they still had to go to get to the doorway, just visible as a darker patch of darkness above them.

Then the next swell of the sea closed the cave off from the late afternoon light. Squeezing each other's cold, gritty hands they silently groped their way onwards.

Felix suddenly cried out, slipping and gasping. Another boom of the sea, and they were both peppered with pinpricks as droplets of ice-cold salt water sprayed across them.

'Felix?' Etta pleaded, feeling around until she felt something clammy and pliable under her fingers. She grabbed it and held on tight; it was Felix's wrist.

'Etta, the water's really high!' Felix coughed shakily. 'My foot went in, it's freezing!'

'It's a full moon,' she replied, trying to sound calm and remember everything she'd read about the sea. 'And spring. The tides are higher at spring, that's all. Give me your other hand and I'll pull you back up.'

With a heave, Etta hauled Felix up to the rock they'd been standing on. She could already feel the waves lapping at her boots.

'We're almost back at the tunnel, Felix,' Etta reassured him. *I hope.* 'You go in front, I'll catch you if you slip.'

They carefully stepped around each other, and carried on, striving always upwards. The baby spiderlings in Etta's hair were doing their best to give them some light, but they were only little and very tired. Their faint glow was comforting though and gave some small shape to the darkness.

All the while, as they struggled up the waves followed, constantly nipping at their heels and spraying them with cold droplets that weighed down their clothes. The crashing and booming were relentless, dulling their exhausted minds.

The children's fingers were so numb with cold they struggled to grip the sharp rocks as they climbed, and more than once Etta wondered if her hands were wet with seawater or blood. She was so cold she didn't think she'd know if she had cut herself.

After crawling and climbing for what felt like forever, Etta looked up and nearly cried with relief to dimly see they were almost at the entrance to the tunnel. They'd be able to make it home in time for dinner.

Just in front, Felix raised himself up on his arms.

Without warning, Marin flew out of the shadows and swooped headfirst down to them, her pale, glowing face halting at the tunnel entrance. Her deep eyes were like holes in the darkness, her face a white death mask against the blackness behind. Her hair and pale dress twisted around her as she rolled, reaching for them weakly, her face spinning before them.

Felix came almost nose to nose with her. He cried out in fright and pushed away, falling backwards onto Etta. Caught unawares, Etta fell down, Felix's hard boot heel coming down on her fingers. She cried out in pain as he lost his footing and fell into the water behind.

The last weak glow from her spiderlings blinked out.

Etta scrabbled around and crawled to the edge of the rock they were on, only to be hit in the face by another icy wave.

'Felix?' she coughed out. 'Felix, where are you?' She'd already lost her bearings completely in the pitch black.

'Et—' she heard, then a frantic coughing and gulping. 'Etta!'

She tried to angle herself towards the choking sounds, her hands outstretched.

'Felix!' Something cold wrapped around her arm, and she flinched away from its damp touch in disgust.

'Etta, it's me!' spluttered Felix.

'Sorry! Are you alright?' They were drenched again by another wave but managed to keep hold of each other this time.

'We just have to climb up a little more, we're almost there!' she shouted over the roar of the waves.

'I'm stuck!' yelled Felix.

'What do you mean stuck?!'

'I'm hooked on something; I can't get free.'

'Where?' Etta stuck one arm into the icy water. She felt around and found some sort of metal hook thing sticking out of the rock. Felix's overlarge jumpers were twisted tight around. *But the waterline on the rocks wasn't this high, we shouldn't be underwater here* . . .

She couldn't hear Felix's gasping breaths anymore.

'Felix?'

There was silence, then exhausted wheezing and splashing in the dark.

'I keep going under,' Felix choked out. 'The water is too high.'

'We've got to get your jumper off,' Etta exclaimed, feeling around to pull his arms out of the sleeves.

'I've tried, it's twisted up too tight. I can hardly move.' There was a gulp and he disappeared under another wave. Etta, holding on tight, was pulled forwards up to her armpits in the brine, coughing out a mouthful of saltwater as she tried to hold on.

Feeling a wretch Etta let go of her cousin to turn her pockets out on the rocks. She blindly fumbled with unfeeling fingers for her pocketknife. It was only a tiny thing, but Mother had sharpened the little blade only a few weeks ago, so Etta could help prune the clematis.

Etta's chest clenched, her heart juddering and her lungs paralysing as the severity of their situation dawned upon her. They were trapped with the rising tide . . . they might never see their parents again.

Forcing a gulp of air into her constricted lungs, Etta ducked under the water, having to grope deeper now, her clothes immediately dragging her down. Blindly she grabbed a handful of wool and pulled it taut so that she could hack at it. Felix was struggling now, his body fighting for air. Etta could barely feel her own fingers gripping the knife, she started to worry that she had actually let go and dropped it. The numbness in her extremities was spreading to her limbs. Everything was cold, except her lungs which started to burn as she frantically sawed, trying to free Felix before they needed another breath.

It was no use, she had to breathe, she was starting to see white dots explode before her eyes. Etta shot up like a cork, and the surface seemed much further away than before. She took a deep breath and couldn't hear Felix at all.

'Felix!' she screamed. 'Felix!'

A warm pair of hands reached under her arms and hauled her back out of the water.

'Felix!' Etta screamed, pushing away and trying to jump back in.

'Hey, hey. Stop. I've got you.' The unfamiliar voice came out of the darkness, raised above the sound of the waves but not shouting. 'We're getting him, calm down. Come back from the edge.'

'He'll drown,' Etta sobbed, suddenly realising she was crying. 'It's all my fault.' Her face stung with salt.

'Shhhh, you're freezing,' he soothed. 'Sit back here.'

Numbly Etta let herself be led backwards and helped up to the rocks above.

'Stop there, before you hit your head. Sit down, I'll be back.'

On some level, Etta vaguely realised that the boy who was helping her must somehow be able to see in the dark. She sat shaking for a moment, her hammering heart louder in her ears than the echoing waves in the cavern. Her chest felt tight, like there was a boulder in it, stopping air from coming easily. Every breath was a fight she gasped and gulped for. Then Etta couldn't bear it any longer and crept tentatively forwards, reaching for the edge.

There was an explosion of water just below her, and a sodden slap of something wet and heavy landing on the rock. Etta groped forwards and fell, landing almost on top of a cold, clammy heap. It wasn't moving.

'Felix?' Etta cried.

CHAPTER 19

'GET OUT OF THE WAY,' SNAPPED A GIRL'S VOICE. Etta felt more movement around her. A warm pair of hands took hers gently, and the voice that had guided her away from the edge earlier spoke quietly.

'Stay quiet now, don't interrupt,' he warned softly.

Etta squeezed the warm hands with her freezing ones. The girl's voice began singing, low and sweet now. The melody was enchanting. It tugged at Etta's feelings, causing her tears to flow faster. A faint glow started to build from the girl's palms, illuminating her. She was maybe a few years older than Etta, bobbing waist deep in the water, holding her hands above Felix's chest. He lay on his back and looked asleep, but his chest wasn't moving. He'd lost the ridiculously large woolly jumpers and was just in his vest and trousers. He lay as still as the mussels that clung to the rocks, so still Etta felt like her heart was shrinking as she watched him.

Pale tendrils of coral light started to grow from the girl's hands, twining softly around her fingers and wrists before stretching

towards Felix's chest. Etta went to put a hand out to him, but her rescuer tightened his grip a little in warning.

Looking at Felix made her cry harder, so Etta looked at the girl instead. She was bathed in the luminous rose glow from her palms. It made her tawny skin and eyes glow as well. Her wet hair was thick black waves, rippling down her front into the sea. She wore bracelets and necklaces of shells and sea glass, mixed with beads, rings, keys, seemingly anything she could thread on a string.

She was staring intently at Felix as she concentrated, controlling her magic. The coral tendrils probed his skin, before slipping into his nose and mouth. Etta's eyes widened and she opened her mouth to protest, to ask what they were doing to him. A boy swam forwards from the darkness to the edge of the pink glow. He had very similar features to the girl.

Brother and sister, Etta thought. The boy noticed her staring and fluttered his golden tail up out of the water teasingly. Etta's mouth fell open in shock at the sight of it, causing him to laugh softly, his grin dazzling.

Abruptly, Felix began coughing up lungfuls of seawater, retching and hiccupping as he rolled onto his side. He almost toppled back into the sea, but the boy in the water swam forwards to hold him.

Etta could see the boy better now. He had long, thick black hair in a strip down the centre of his golden-brown scalp, plaited through with tiny shells and beads, and cascading down over one shoulder. A single jewel hung down in the centre of his forehead, stopping just above and between his thick, black eyebrows. One of those eyebrows had a golden ring pierced through it.

Both siblings had eyes outlined in black – hers topaz, his storm grey – and they were both bestrewn with jewels and shells: sparkling bracelets, necklaces, rings and earrings adorned their brown skin.

The stranger's hands released hers, and Etta turned to see who they belonged to.

'I'm Ronan,' said the boy behind her quietly.

He clearly wasn't one of the merfolk; he had legs, in pale grey moleskin trousers. The two mer were golden, glossy and beautiful. This boy was drab in comparison, with shaggy brown hair streaked with grey, in spite of him being close to her own age.

But then mine is white, reasoned Etta. Like the mer, Ronan didn't seem to feel the cold, while Etta was shivering.

Felix's teeth were also chattering as he sat up in his soaked vest. Ronan was bare-chested, his grey shirt bunched down around his waist. He was almost camouflaged against the rocks, barely visible. The only noteworthy thing about him was his eyes: they were long-lashed and liquid black, like the eyes of a seal.

'Dry them out, Wyn, before they freeze to death,' the mer boy suggested from the water.

The girl looked at him archly and waved a hand behind her.

'I rather think I'm doing plenty already.'

Etta looked past them to see what she meant and saw the waves crashing against an invisible barrier, like they were enclosed in a safe little bubble. She looked at Felix and met his eyes, which were as big and round as hers.

W O W, Felix mouthed.

'They can't take the cold like we can. Please, Aerwynna?' Ronan pleaded.

The mer girl rolled her eyes, then held out her hands towards Etta and Felix. Etta noticed she had delicate webs between her fingers, and her nails were dark and curved, like claws.

'I can't make you warm,' Aerwynna stated. 'I only have power over water. I can remove it from your clothes like I took it from his lungs. You'll be dry, but getting warm is your problem.'

It was the strangest feeling – Etta's clothes felt as though they were crawling with spiderlings. At first, she couldn't see anything, just peach curls of light weaving through her jumper. Then tiny water droplets began to form, hanging suspended all around her, and Felix too. They got bigger and bigger, and joined together, until Aerwynna had a sphere of water hovering above them, coral tendrils of light forming a shimmering cage around it.

'It's beautiful,' Etta breathed.

Aerwynna looked a trifle smug as she undulated her tail,

taking her backwards away from the ledge, the ball of water floating above her cupped hands. Then she abruptly splayed out her hands, throwing her magic wide and dropping the whole water sphere onto her brother's head.

'Ugh! You dragonfish!' he yelled, outraged, while she fell about in peals of laughter.

'Well,' said Ronan dryly. 'That's the twins, Aerwynna and Finn.' He shook his head, smiling a little. 'How are you both feeling?'

'Much better for being dry, thank you,' said Felix, through chattering teeth. Etta took off her topmost jumper and passed it to him.

'How did you . . . ?' Felix waved his hands at the ceiling of the bubble they were in, where Aerwynna's magic looped and curled, bathing them in soft, carmine light.

'I'm a siren,' she said, in a superior tone.

Her brother shook his head.

'I'm not,' he said with a grin.

'What does it mean, being a siren?' asked Etta.

'A siren is a mer who can communicate with elements or sea life. We can use our song to manipulate something. In my case, it's water, but some sirens can move rocks, or control sea creatures, or plants.'

'That's just like our—' Felix began, but Etta suddenly pulled him to her in a fierce hug.

'Felix! I was so worried about you!' she cried loudly, then hissed low into his ear. 'Don't tell them who we are!'

Etta had meant the hug as a way of stopping Felix revealing their identity, but she became unexpectedly overwhelmed by her own emotions. She pulled away, but not completely, keeping her arm around Felix's shoulders as more of her tears spilled.

'I thought you, that we . . .' she started.

'I know,' Felix whispered. He put his arm around her. 'I did too.'

'How did you two get in the cave?' asked Ronan. 'You can only access it by boat at low tide.'

'We . . .' Etta paused, thinking fast. 'We got lost in the woods, and . . . and a ghost scared us. We somehow ended up down here.'

'A ghost?' Ronan leaned forwards eagerly. 'What did it look like?'

'Pale and see-through,' Etta laughed weakly, and exchanged a look with Felix. They'd both noticed that Marin looked a lot like Ronan, the same dappling on the skin, the enormous black eyes. Ronan was waiting expectantly for more. 'Er . . . long dark hair, big, dark eyes, like yours.'

Felix pointed up. 'She's inside that tunnel, just there.'

Everyone looked towards the black doorway. No one spoke for a moment, then Aerwynna glared at them, her eyes cold and hard.

'How did you get inside that tunnel?'

There was a long silence as they all looked at Etta.

'The entrance to the other end of that tunnel is in a private estate,' Finn continued in his amiable tone, but with a watchfulness to his eyes now, a sense that he knew where this was going and he really didn't like it. 'If you didn't know it was there, you'd not be able to find it. It's enchanted.'

Etta and Felix sat closer and hugged each other tighter, not meeting anyone's gaze.

'Where, exactly, do you live?' asked Finn quietly, a hard edge creeping into his voice.

Keeping her arm tightly around Felix, Etta pointed behind them, towards Stitchwort.

'You . . .' Ronan spluttered. 'You're one of them? That family of thieves and plunderers?'

'What?' cried Etta indignantly. 'No, I am not! We,' she indicated herself and Felix, 'are from a family of famous scientists and artists.'

Ronan, Finn and Aerwynna stared at each other, then burst out in peals of cruel laughter.

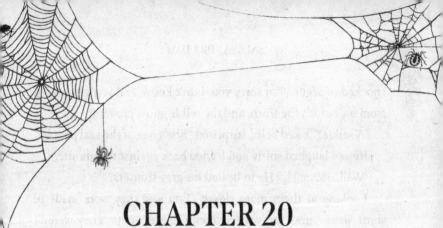

CHAPTER 20

A S THEIR LAUGHTER DIED AWAY, RONAN'S nostrils were flared and his mouth set in a bitter line.

'I never would have helped you, if I'd known.'

Finn scoffed.

'You'd never let kids drown. Even if they are from *that* family,' he said quietly, patting Ronan's leg soothingly.

Etta's head jerked up angrily.

'What's wrong with my family?'

Ronan scowled at her. 'They're a bunch of thieving, murdering witches – that's what's wrong.'

Etta scowled right back.

'And who are we supposed to have murdered then?' she demanded.

'My great-great-grandmother,' Ronan replied coolly. 'That ghost you saw? Trapped in your wreck of a house? She was murdered by your ancestors.'

Finn and Aerwynna nodded as well.

'It's true,' Finn agreed. Etta and Felix looked at him, too

shocked to argue. 'I'm sorry you didn't know, and you've heard it from us, but it's the truth, and the selkie ghost proves it.'

'A selkie?' asked Felix, surprised. 'She's one of the seal people?'

Ronan laughed softly and leaned back against the granite.

'Well, obviously.' He indicated his grey trousers.

Looking at them more closely, Etta saw they were made of short, dense, grey fur, scattered with lighter spots. They weren't separate from the top as she'd first assumed, but a complete garment, like her father's winter all-in-one underwear. Ronan had slipped his arms out of the pelt, leaving the top part bunched around his waist.

Leaning to look behind him, Etta saw the seal head lying like an empty hood on the rocks. She could see the pale inside of the face, like a hollow mask. Etta shuddered.

Ronan looked behind him as well.

'Yes, that's my sealskin. When I slip into it, I'll be in my seal body, and I'll swim out of here with these two jellyfish brains.'

'Hey!' objected Finn, flicking water at Ronan.

'Why do you think our ancestors killed Marin?' asked Felix.

Ronan looked surprised.

'How do you know her name?' he asked.

Etta leaned back as well, mirroring Ronan's relaxed pose.

'We met her for the first time earlier today,' she began casually. 'She was trapped, and we freed her. She asked us to help her, and we're going to.' She finished, making it sound like a challenge.

'And how are you going to do that?' asked Aerwynna acidly.

'Wynn,' her brother cautioned. 'They're just kids.'

Felix cleared his throat. 'She wants us to help her find

something,' he said. 'But we don't know what.'

Understanding dawned on Etta, and she sat forwards eagerly.

'"Find the rest of me" – her sealskin, Felix. She wants us to find her sealskin!' She looked to Ronan for confirmation. 'That's right, isn't it?'

He nodded slowly, narrowing his eyes at them.

'But how did she lose it in the first place?' asked Felix, puzzled.

Ronan gave a humourless laugh.

'She didn't lose it; it was taken from her. By your family.'

'Can you prove that?' asked Etta bitingly.

Ronan sat up.

'If she'd died in an accident, they'd have returned her body to us. Everyone knows your family thought they were great pioneers in every field. Benita's speciality was studying magical objects; she obviously took the sealskin.'

'And that's not all they took,' interjected Aerwynna. 'Your family plundered their way around the globe, taking whatever they fancied from anywhere they landed and stuffing their pockets with priceless artefacts and relics. When they were quite finished ransacking the land . . .'

'They started on the sea,' finished Finn quietly, not meeting Etta or Felix's eyes. 'And other realms.'

'Why would they do that?' asked Etta, trying to sound curious and not defensive. Felix gave her shoulder a little squeeze of sympathy. 'My ancestors were artists and plant hunters, people who made great discoveries, they drew maps and discovered new medicines. They weren't thieves and murderers.'

'Well,' said Finn diplomatically. 'Maybe it's different sides of

the same fish. You've been told your family made great discoveries, but you weren't told at what cost.'

Etta reached for Felix's hand, thinking of the poor horses and Harold, who'd lost his life in the Orinoco River.

'Maybe,' she admitted quietly, looking up at the luminescent coral bubble that surrounded them. The waves crashed against it, almost halfway up the sides, but the bubble protected them from the angry sea, and muffled the noise of it.

'I can't hold it for much longer,' Aerwynna said. 'I could, if our ancestors hadn't been tricked and robbed as well.'

'Something was taken from you too?' asked Etta, her shoulders sinking under the weight of her shame.

'The Mermaid's Eye,' Aerwynna declared.

Felix screwed up his face. 'Oh, that's disgusting!'

Aerwynna rolled her golden eyes expressively. 'It's not an actual eyeball. Are you as stupid as a sunfish? It's a pearl, about this big.' She cupped her hands as if she were holding a large apple. 'We use it for powerful magic, deep under the sea. The Eye gives sirens a stronger connection to the divine energy of the moon.'

She saw Felix gaping at her blankly and flicked her fins irritably.

'I can manipulate water, but the strength of the moon on tides and winds is too great. I cannot calm a storm, divert a tide. I can't protect our community without channelling the moon's power. I need the Eye to do that. We want it back,' she stated firmly, folding her arms and flicking her tail side to side to hold her position in the pool.

'We *need* it back. The Eye has been out of the sea for so long now it'll be dying, and with it go our remaining defences. Haven't you noticed the weather here getting worse over the years? Our elders have been talking about leaving this bay, leaving our home! But it's no safer anywhere else, with your war machines and explosions polluting the oceans. We're not safe anywhere there are humans. There's talk of all mer clans retreating to the furthest depths of the oceans, so we have no contact with your toxic species.'

Aerwynna grimaced, as though she were holding back tears. Then she scowled at Felix again.

'There's been big cliff falls here too. The Eye dying affects you on land as well. We protect you from the weather as much as we do ourselves.'

Aerwynna suddenly splayed a webbed hand across her chest and the pink luminescence around them faded, like the glow from Etta's spiderlings earlier. Finn frowned, coming close to his sister.

'You've done too much this afternoon. Let's get home for some rest. It's nearly dinnertime.' He looked up at Ronan, still sitting on the rock ledge, and jerked his head in Etta and Felix's direction. 'Will you take them home?'

Ronan smirked. 'Well, you can't, can you? Codfish.'

Finn flicked water at him. 'Goblin shark!'

Aerwynna rolled her eyes and cupped some seawater into her hands. She blew on it gently and the water swirled into a ball, hovering above her palm. She hummed a note and it pulsed, then glowed a tranquil sea green. She held the light out to Ronan, who cupped his hand under the ball as he stood up.

Ronan turned to Etta and Felix.

'We need to get you two up there before Wynn's big bubble

bursts,' he said, indicating for them to climb up before him. 'And you can introduce me to my great-great-grandmother.'

Etta helped Felix over the lip of the ledge, then moved to the side so she could examine where the edge of the bubble touched the wall, like a curved piece of stained glass. Rainbows shimmered within it. Turning to look down at the twins, they could see the waves churning angrily against the outside.

'We'd have drowned here for sure,' Felix whispered quietly to Etta, squeezing her hand. She pulled him into a fierce hug.

'Thank you,' Felix called down.

Ronan waved to the twins with the light. They waved back before diving; a flick of their sparkling golden scales and they were gone. A moment later, the coral glow winked out, the swirling tendrils of Aerwynna's magic following her back into the ocean. The wall of water came crashing in, the roar of the freed waves so frighteningly loud that Etta and Felix staggered back into the dark doorway.

Ronan shook his head, holding the light high as he watched the water crash and thunder in up to his ankles.

'I've never seen a spring tide this high before,' he commented. 'I wonder what brought it on.'

'Our curse,' replied Etta, as she turned to face the darkness.

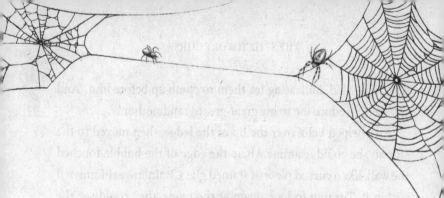

CHAPTER 21

'WHAT CURSE?' RONAN ASKED, AS THEY began to climb the path to the surface.

Etta gaped at him and exchanged a glance with Felix. 'The curse! The Stitchwort Curse! Our whole family was cursed by all of you! After the fire, everyone outside of Stitchwort died, except Benita and her direct descendants. Some of them in very peculiar circumstances.'

'I have no idea what you're talking about,' said Ronan impatiently. 'Look, I've got to get you pups back safely and see my ghostly great-great-grandmother!' He held the light up and pointed ahead. 'Walk faster.'

'Have you ever been up here before?' asked Felix as they started up the rough-hewn steps.

'Years ago,' Ronan replied. 'We thought we could find out the truth about what happened to our missing clanswoman. But we couldn't get past the exit at the top. It was like there was an invisible wall there. A binding spell preventing entry.'

'We?' asked Felix.

Ronan grinned. 'A group of other selkie pups and me. We dared each other to break into the house and search for clues. We were taking running jumps and kicks at the open doorway, trying to break through.' He laughed at the memory. 'But that binding spell holds firm. And after all this time too – someone did an excellent job of it.'

Etta drifted behind, walking slower than the others, lost in her spinning thoughts.

'Etta!' called Felix. 'Hurry up.'

'I still don't understand,' Etta said to Ronan as she reached them. 'The selkies haven't cursed us?'

Ronan shook his head.

'My ancestors swore never to help any of you again if you were wrecked, and to terrorise you if you came down to the beach. The mer swore revenge – taking one of their sacred Eyes angered the whole mer community worldwide. It was like a missing link in a chain, it affected the balance of the seas. The local mer were screeching for Starling blood. There are several sirens in the clan here, they would have been able to use the Eye to amplify their powers. The loss of it has badly affected their fortunes.'

'In what way?' asked Felix.

Ronan sighed. 'Well, Finn doesn't brag about it much, but he's a gifted healer. His ancestors developed an incredible garden of medicinal plants down there. He's apprentice healer to his grandfather. Decades ago, the storms up here caused a landslide and some of the cliff fell into the sea. They could have prevented it with the Eye. The landslide crushed their garden; they lost some very rare and ancient plants. They used to make medicines for other mer communities, sea life and selkies too. Without the Eye, the sirens have been unable to move all the rock. Some was moveable by hand, and we selkies helped as much as we could too. Finn and his grandfather have been rebuilding the garden, they can cure most things again now. But some of what was lost is irreplaceable.'

Felix gave a low whistle. 'No wonder they hate us.'

Ronan nodded. 'That might be why you think you're cursed. The mer wanted their Eye back. With the house abandoned they assumed one of the Starlings must have it, so they wrecked any Starling ship they could find – wrecked and pillaged it, like the one down there in the cave. They sent out a call to all the mer worldwide for help.'

Etta frowned. 'That would explain the deaths at sea, but there were some very odd ones that happened on land as well.' She turned to Felix. 'Like Francis Starling – he was captured by pirates! He escaped, but then he was attacked by a moon bear in the Himalayas. He escaped the bear but after all that, he was devoured by crocodiles in a mangrove forest. Such a series of events can't possibly occur by mere accident. He was hunted down by the curse!'

Before Felix could reply, they heard a sob in the darkness ahead.

'Marin?' called Felix gently. Ronan held the glowing light up and the ghost swam into view. Etta smiled, now she understood why the ghost always looked to be swimming through the air – it was her selkie nature coming through. Seeing Marin's seal-like black eyes and dappled skin again, Etta wondered how she had ever mistaken her for a human housemaid.

Ronan inhaled sharply at the sight of her.

'She looks so much like my mother,' he marvelled, lowering the light.

His gasp drew Marin's attention and she drifted closer, head swaying as she tried to see him past Etta and Felix. Ronan pushed himself between them and came forwards.

'H-hello,' he said haltingly. 'I'm Ronan, I'm your great-great-grandson.'

Marin's face creased with distress.

It's been ... that long?

She moaned and covered her face with her hands. Etta felt a wave of sadness. Marin hadn't realised how long she'd been dead for. She'd missed her children and grandchildren growing up.

'Whoever did this, they stole much more than treasure,' Etta growled at Felix.

He nodded back grimly. 'We can't fix everything, but we'll do what we can.'

'We tried to get your sealskin back,' Ronan explained, holding his hands up to her in an almost pleading gesture. 'We tried to come up here, to find you, but we couldn't get in. You were never forgotten.'

'This tunnel is probably the only place they can meet, between her tether to her skin and the binding spell that keeps him out,' muttered Etta to Felix.

'Not for long,' promised Felix.

Marin was following the curves of Ronan's face with a ghostly finger, smiling when she saw a little of her own bloodline in his features.

'Marin?' called Etta softly. 'Felix and I will find your sealskin and we'll give it back to Ronan. But do you know where they hid it? Who took it from you? Was it Benita Starling? Do you remember?'

She walked forwards, to stand beside Ronan in the damp, narrow corridor.

'If you know what they did with it, we can find it faster and get you back home.'

Marin stared at Etta for a long time, in the darkness of the corridor her eyes were pits of sucking black. Etta longed to flinch away, but forced herself to stay brave.

Not . . . Benita

'It wasn't Benita who took your sealskin?' Ronan asked.

Benita . . . friend

Etta stared at her.

'What? Are you perhaps confused?'

Edgar thief . . . Benita friend

Etta looked back at Felix, who was as dumbfounded as she was. All three of them turned back to the ghost.

'Edgar was the head of the family,' Etta spoke slowly, patiently. 'He was a respected gentleman and a scholar. He ran the estate and cared for his younger sister.'

Ronan cleared his throat, playing the ball of light across his fingers to avoid looking at Etta.

'Well, Benita was the scholar. He was more about drinking and card games, from the stories I've heard . . .'

'Those stories,' Etta replied frostily, 'are over a century old and have no doubt been twisted and embellished.'

Marin nodded slowly. Then:

Edgar a thief ... Benita my friend

This time there was a note of determination in her voice as it slipped through Etta's mind, the immovable rock under the swaying sea.

Etta sighed, and muttered to Felix.

'Maybe Benita Starling pretended to be her friend to dupe her out of the sealskin. Marin must not have realised before she died.' She looked back at the ghost who was gazing adoringly at her great-great-grandson's face. 'Let's get you back home, Marin. You can't haunt a damp passageway forever.'

She turned to Ronan. 'I promise we'll do our best to find out the truth and find the sealskin.'

Ronan nodded slowly, still staring at the ghost. 'How am I going to explain this to my family?' he asked, with a dark chuckle.

'Tell them we'll search the whole house, I promise. Every room, every drawer. We won't stop until we find the sealskin, and the Eye, and return them,' Etta promised earnestly.

Ronan took a last look at Marin, then held out the light.

'We're nearly at the top,' he said. 'Would you like this to get the rest of the way?'

Felix held out a hand and took the little light.

'Don't you need it?' he asked, rolling the ball from one hand to the other.

Ronan shook his head and flashed them a grin. 'Seals can see quite well in the dark, you know.'

155

Etta searched the sky as they left the passageway.

'The sun's down. Drat.'

'Do you think we missed dinner?' asked Felix wistfully, his stomach growling loudly as he thought of Etta's father's wonderful meals.

Etta looked down at herself and across at her cousin. They were both noticeably bashed up, with cuts and scrapes all over them. They were dry, at least, but Felix had lost both of his jumpers and Etta's were looking very much the worse for wear. She started leading the way back towards the house, Marin bobbing along dreamily behind them.

'I try to avoid lying, it only causes more problems later on,' she said. 'But if we tell them the truth, we'll be shut in the Herbarium with Grandfather for weeks, doing extra lessons so they can keep an eye on us.'

'What do we do then?' asked Felix. 'We promised we'd look for the sealskin and the Eye. We can't be locked up!'

Etta grimaced. 'We'll have to dance around the edges of the truth . . .' She stopped, holding a hand up as they saw a light ahead.

'Marin!' she hissed. 'Quick, hide!'

Silently, Marin drifted back into the snowy tree trunks, her pale dress camouflaging perfectly.

'Over here!' called Viola, running towards them with a lantern held high. 'I've found them.'

She ran straight to Felix and roughly inspected him, interrogating him rapidly in Dutch before clasping him in a hug. He rolled his eyes widely against her shoulder and looked to Etta for help.

'I'm so sorry, Mrs Grey,' Etta began, as her mother reached them, her eyes sweeping over the children. 'We came outside to play but went too far in the woods and lost track of the time. It grew dark and we got turned around in the trees and headed in the wrong direction. We were stuck . . .' she tailed off, as Mother's eyes were narrowing shrewdly. She didn't look very convinced.

Etta gave up trying to be brave for Felix and let the exhaustion sweep over her. She sagged, almost wailing.

'We're so cold! And hungry! I'm really sorry, we'll stay indoors tomorrow.' She sniffed and rubbed her eyes on her sleeve. Mother looked more sympathetic now. 'Please can we sit by the fire and have some dinner? I'm sorry we're late.'

'You're not very late,' Mother said. She glanced between them. 'Well, as long as neither of you are hurt. Come along then.' She turned and let the way back to the house.

'Wait, that's it?' called Viola, hurrying after her. 'We haven't known where they've been or what they've been doing for hours. I was worried sick!' Her voice faded as she chased after Mary.

'Dinner and bed,' Felix yawned. 'I think I'll sleep until lunchtime tomorrow!'

'Absolutely not,' Etta objected. 'We've a sealskin to find.'

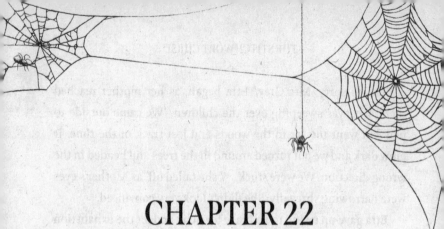

CHAPTER 22

ETTA SMILED AND PUT HER NOTEBOOK DOWN when the knock came on her tree trunk late the next morning. Her tree expanded a doorway and Felix slipped inside.

'You were ages!' she complained. 'How was your papa?'

Felix grinned. Although he'd looked tired at breakfast, after their cave adventure, his eyes were bright and he couldn't stop smiling.

'Papa's up and out of bed! Mama's taking him for a walk in the garden now. Your grandmother has exercises for him to do every day, to build up his strength, and your father is baking special meals to help him be strong and healthy again.' Felix beamed as he told Etta the final piece of news. 'He wants his instruments, and he wants to see the music room here!'

'That's wonderful!' exclaimed Etta. 'Although if he knew what the music room looked like, he wouldn't be asking to see it! It's dusty sheets covering out-of-tune instruments, and a jackdaw's nest has collapsed down into the fireplace.'

Felix laughed.

'Not for long! My violin lessons will start up again soon, and he'd like to teach you something as well.'

Etta thought it over as she sent her spiders lowering two bags down to Felix. She'd tried to learn the piano from books before but had got stuck when the sheet music became more complicated.

'Can he teach me piano?' she asked tentatively.

'Of course.' Felix smiled as he watched the bags reach the floor. 'What are these?'

'Last time we had one bag of food and equipment, which we've temporarily misplaced,' Etta began.

'Lost,' corrected Felix. 'I would like my torch back one day.'

'Temporarily misplaced,' Etta argued, as she climbed nimbly down the ladder. 'I will get it back. Either those tangles can start listening to me or they'll have to go! I'm not being kept out of my own home.' She picked one of the bags up and placed it over her shoulder determinedly.

Felix sighed and gave up arguing. 'Today we have a bag each?'

'I thought it would be prudent to have a spare,' Etta explained. 'They're both packed with the same food and equipment.'

'And where are we taking this food and equipment?' Felix hesitated, still not picking his bag up. 'I'm not going back into those ruins. Not with those tangles.'

'We're not going in the ruins,' Etta reassured him, as she waited for the bedroom doorway to open for her. 'We're going to find the truth.'

'We got that yesterday. Hey!' Felix exclaimed as he stepped out to see Etta squeezing past her tree in the direction of the ruined wing. 'You said we weren't going back in there!'

'We're not going as far as Edgar's parlour,' Etta insisted. 'I promise. And we didn't get the truth yesterday. We got a century-old fairy story that's been told and retold, adding rumours and gossip and becoming a ridiculous legend. They didn't even know anyone still lived in our house!'

'Marin said Benita was her friend,' Felix pointed out. He searched the ceiling. 'Where is Marin anyway?'

Etta felt her cheeks flush.

'I fetched her back from the woods, then she was bobbing around in my tree all night. I couldn't get to sleep,' she said. 'So, I sent her away.'

'Away?'

'Well, I couldn't let her wander the house alone! I asked if she visited Stitchwort often, and she said yes. I asked what her favourite room was and . . .' Etta paused. 'Well, here we are.'

Felix looked at the door, barely clinging on to its frame.

'You left her in the bat tower?'

Etta gave the door a gentle push and watched it topple forward, only for the final twisted hinge to halt it mid-air. She pointed up.

Marin was looping the loop above them, watching the bats hanging from the remaining bits of the ceiling. She swam through a window opening and circled around the broken outer wall, coming in beside Felix and weaving between them with a smile.

Etta shrugged. 'Apparently, she likes bats.'

Fluffy . . . Marin agreed.

'So, are we looking for . . .' Felix hesitated, checking how close Marin was, '. . . her sealskin?' he whispered.

Etta nodded. She looked down at the canopy below, the snow covering the treetops.

'I had some thoughts last night, when she wanted to come here. Marin?' she called.

The ghost rippled towards them, her plain dress billowing as she flowed through the air.

Etta sat down in the doorway, dangling her legs over the drop.

'Marin, was this room a bedroom?'

Yes

'Was it Benita Starling's bedroom?'

The ghost looped around, smiling.

Yes

'Benita was your friend?'

Yes

'Are we ever getting more than a one-word answer out of her?' Felix grumbled, leaning against the doorway behind Etta.

'I thought at first she was a little scrambled from being trapped in the cobwebs for so long, but I've been wondering if it's because she's not whole,' Etta reasoned. 'A part of her, a big part, is missing.'

'So, how are we going to find it?' asked Felix. 'Searching this house could take years!'

'I would dearly love to search Benita's bedroom,' Etta leaned forwards a little, peeping over her knees to look down at the treetops. 'Sadly, I think we'll have to wait until the snow has melted.' She sighed and sat back.

'From everything I've read about selkies, if they take their skin off to walk on land in their other form, they hide the skin. They always hide it well. They can't get too far from it, and they can't return to the sea without it. They lose their seal form. But Marin must have brought the skin with her, to show either Edgar or Benita Starling, for them to study. She trusted them.'

Felix knelt beside her.

'Do you think it was in the parlour? It'll be destroyed if it was, and we'll never be able to free her.'

Etta shook her head.

'The parlour was an entertaining space, somewhere Edgar would have had his friends over to display his fancy collections and, I don't know, drink brandy or whatever they all did together. Lots of late-night boasting! The skin would have been taken to a workroom, or a study – somewhere with equipment.'

Felix looked along the corridor, at the boarded-up rooms.

'Your parents didn't break into many of these, did they? Just the first few. When they didn't find anything useful, they gave up?'

Etta nodded, her curls bobbing.

'Marin,' she called to the ghost again. 'Marin, do you remember which room you brought your sealskin to? To show your friend?'

The ghost stopped her circuits of the ruins and hovered in the centre of the tower, looking down. Her long hair covered her face, and she wrapped her arms around herself.

'I'm sorry,' Etta whispered. 'I know it's painful, but we want to help you find it. If we start in the last place you remember having it . . .'

You will not see

'We'll try,' Felix reassured her. 'We'll try our hardest to find it.'

Marin looked up at them, her face dismal with grief and loss. Shoulders slumped, she drifted forwards, the buoyancy drained from her flight. Etta and Felix quickly scrambled out of the doorway, so she didn't drift through them, and followed her along the darkened hallway.

Marin floated straight through a section of wall, leaving Etta and Felix outside. Etta grinned fiercely, passing Felix a candle and hefting her crowbar.

'I knew I'd be needing this today,' she crowed.

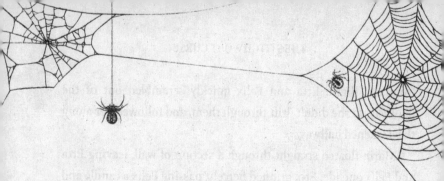

CHAPTER 23

ETTA PLANTED HER FEET FIRMLY AND WEDGED the crowbar against a hairline crack in the wall.

'Ready?' she asked Felix, who was close behind, poised to add his weight to the crowbar.

'You're sure it's a secret door?' asked Felix. 'Marin might have just floated off outside.'

Etta knocked against the wall, the sound loud and hollow.

'We knocked all around this area, Felix,' she reminded him. 'This panel here is hollow, it must be a door. A *secret* door, leading to untold wonders!' She laughed, opening her eyes wide.

Felix picked at the crumbling dado rail that ran along the hallway.

'Are we going to get in trouble for breaking in?' he worried.

Ignoring him, Etta took up her position again.

Felix flinched back, then held his hand near the wall. A pale spot of light flickered across his palm.

'Look!' he called out. 'What is it?' he asked, as the light vanished.

Etta let go of the crowbar and it thudded to the floor, hitting the faded runner with a flat, metallic sound.

'I never get to use my crowbar,' she grumbled.

Shaking her head ruefully, Etta crouched so her nose was almost touching the wall, bringing her eye against a well-hidden keyhole. Through it she could make out a room, and the flitting form of Marin flying around it. When the ghost passed close to the keyhole her light shone out into the dark hallway, dancing across Etta's face.

Etta sat back. Concentrating, she reached out with her mind, searching for her bedroom and the spiders gathered there. Etta pictured where she was, and what she needed. They were reluctant to venture down into the dangerous ruined wing, but she clenched her jaw and tugged firmly at the connection between them. A moment later, Etta stood, turning to Felix with a satisfied expression.

'They're coming,' she stated, leaning her crowbar up against the wall.

'I thought your spiders didn't come down here,' Felix commented.

'They don't want to. Apparently, decades ago some of them *did* have a little run in with the tangles while searching for great-aunt Myrtle. They had a heck of a time getting away. That's why they avoid this wing. I've promised them the tangles are only in the burnt-out parlour, not here.'

A soft rustling noise came from the end of the corridor, like a velvet cloth sliding off a table. Holding up their candle, Etta smiled as a group of her fluffy little jumping spiders crept tentatively towards them. Their movements were fast and jerky, almost birdlike. When they reached the circle of light, several came forward and waved their front legs in the air, holding keys.

'Where'd they find those?' asked Felix, crouching down for a closer look.

'My bedroom ceiling,' Etta replied. 'Over the years they've brought me several keys, I never thought to wonder why. Maybe they knew these keys were important?' She laughed. 'I just thought it was because I like pretty shiny things!'

'You should have been a magpie, not a Starling,' Felix joked.

Etta tried the first key in the lock and wiggled it about, with no luck. With every key they tried, she felt a mounting sense of anticipation. Finally, there came a click. It was stiff and slow, but the key turned a full rotation.

Etta seized the handle and looked at Felix, her eyes sparkling with excitement.

'Ready?'

Felix gripped the candle and nodded eagerly. Etta took a deep breath, and turned the door handle.

Marin glowed as she languidly swooped around the perimeter of a large, well-proportioned room with a high ceiling. The ghost seemed content, almost joyful, as she looped and twirled around the furniture.

'Marin seems happy enough,' Etta observed, following the ghost's progress so she could make out the room's layout. 'I'll take that as a sign there's no tangles present.'

Felix peered inside a teacup resting on a nearby table.

'Ugh, don't look in there!' he recoiled, placing the candle as far from it as possible.

Etta waved her hand around to disperse the musty smell as they made their way to the tall windows. They hauled apart the heavy brocade curtains, allowing weak daylight to filter into the room. The dust cloud they created was as thick as soup, but as it dispersed, the light illuminated walls of tall bookshelves accessible by ladders, a pair of deep velvet wingback chairs before a beautifully ornate fireplace, a writing desk in front of the window and, in the centre, a long table covered in tarnished scientific instruments. Some of the beakers contained the dried residue of old experiments, one even looked to have burnt. Dead plants with papery brown leaves were everywhere, large ones in pots on the floor, smaller ones clustered on the window ledges, and even some suspended from the ceiling. The bookshelves were filled with thick leatherbound academic texts and clothbound journals.

'Was it someone's study?' Felix whispered, looking at the long table of complex equipment. Under the dust were neatly stacked notebooks and stout textbooks, precisely marked with scraps of paper.

'It certainly looks that way,' Etta replied quietly. It didn't seem a place for speaking above a whisper.

They carefully inspected rows of glass bottles and jars, their browning labels illegibly marked by faded ink. Some still contained liquid, others were full of powders or organic matter.

'Look,' whispered Etta, brushing the dust from an open notebook. 'See how neat the handwriting is, and how precisely the diagrams are drawn? This doesn't seem like the sort of person who would let their experiment dry out and be ruined.'

'You think it was a Starling who died suddenly, from the curse?' Felix asked.

Etta clenched her fists up under her chin and did a little dance on the spot.

'I think it's *Edgar* Starling's study!' she squealed with glee. 'All the neat labels, drawings and research notes . . . it must be! I'd given up searching for it, I thought it must have been lost in the ruined wing. This is it, Felix! The key to solving everything!'

Felix grinned back.

'We should look at these.' He pointed at the curling sketches pinned up behind the desk. The drawings were fascinating, even through a layer of dust: how to identify a dragon's species from its egg, how to determine a phoenix's age from its feathers, detailed illustrations of strange, unheard-of plants and their properties.

'Look!' Etta tapped a page of botanical sketches. 'These are underwater plants: samphire, sea holly, bladderwrack. But there are others here I've never heard of.'

Felix held the corner of another page.

'These are recipes for potions and cures you can make with them,' he told her. 'And look at all this on the desk.'

The desk had little shelves at the back, filled with pots of seeds, bottles, several hagstones, shells and fossils.

They moved on to the bookshelves, where journals were tightly wrapped in thick, cobweb shrouds. Etta struggled to release them, scratching with her nails and even trying a pair of pliers from one of her deep pockets.

'Ugh!' she grunted, throwing another book to the floor and creating a plume of dust. She was ankle-deep in a fog caused by her futile book-wrestling.

'They must be spelled shut with the spiderwebs!' she fumed, resisting the urge to kick the books in frustration.

Felix stood by the window, tilting a sketchbook to the light to read the soft, curling handwriting.

'What do you expect to find in them anyway?' he asked. 'It'll just be old science notes or diaries.'

'Those diaries might tell us what happened here all those years ago!'

Felix laughed.

'You think our great-great-uncle was writing about his murder while it was happening?' He struck a pose, holding an imaginary pen and affecting a British accent. 'Tuesday the twenty-third of October, 1818. My dear sister is advancing upon me with an axe. I fear I may not finish eating my crumpets.' He backed away from Etta, pretending to write while looking fearful.

Etta glared, her arms folded crossly.

'Finished?' she asked tartly, but she couldn't help her mouth twitching a little. 'These diaries might explain their relationship, the events leading up to the fire, the curse and everything!'

She frowned at the wall behind Felix. He'd backed up to the pair of velvet chairs by the fireplace. There was a small table between them, just big enough for a tea tray. Above the empty grate hung a large picture frame, obscured by dust and darkness. Marin was circling above Felix, amused by his antics. By the glow of the ghost's light, Etta had seen a flash of the painting.

Etta pushed one of the wingback chairs up to the fireplace and stood on it. She held their candle up to the painting.

'Felix!' she cried. 'It's a painting of Benita! It's beautiful – he must have been utterly devoted to her.'

Felix came closer, to scrutinise the painting. Through the thick dust, a girl who looked remarkably like Etta stared back at them. Etta took her handkerchief and began to gently wipe some of the grime off the top of the canvas.

'She looks very like you,' Felix said. Benita had looser white ringlets than Etta, and even paler skin. Her eyes were piercing blue instead of brown, her gaze directed out at the viewer. One hand was up to her mouth, a finger pressed against her lips like she was shushing them. Her other hand rested on her lap, caging a large blue spider with delicate white markings.

Felix started pushing the dirt away from the bottom part of the painting with his own handkerchief.

'I think she was older than me here,' Etta remarked. She noticed Felix had paused. 'Are you alright?'

'I'm getting that feeling again,' Felix stepped back from the painting. 'Like there's something here.'

'On the frame maybe?' Etta leaned back a little to look for cobwebs. 'It's a strange picture, isn't it? Why did he paint her like she was telling us to be quiet?'

'Or she's saying she has a secret?' suggested Felix. He reached out and swept the lower corner clean, then spoke quietly.

'Etta.'

Etta looked down to where Felix was pointing, at the artist signature in the bottom corner. Where the painting was signed *Benita Starling* in a looping, curling script.

Etta stared at it, frowning.

'So, they could both paint,' she said. 'There are many artists in our family, my grandad is very good. Maybe she did it for her brother as a gift?'

Felix nodded. 'But Etta, look . . .' he pointed again at the handwriting. 'It matches the notebooks and drawings.'

Etta froze, staring at the signature.

'Benita was a scholar as well? No one ever mentioned *that* before.' Etta stared at the face that was so like her own. 'There's so much still to learn about them both.'

'It looks like she could command spiders as well, doesn't it?'

'Maybe. My grandfather said his sister had the same hair as me and she had that ability too,' said Etta. She put out a finger and gently stroked the blue tarantula on Benita's lap, then leapt back, stumbling down from the chair.

'Did you see that?' she cried, clutching Felix's arm.

'No, see what?'

'The spider. It moved!'

CHAPTER 24

FELIX LAUGHED.

'Don't be ridiculous, it's painted.'

Etta still felt shocked, her fists clenched.

'Look,' Felix said reassuringly, and poked the painting's surface. Immediately he staggered back.

'Did you hear that?' he cried.

Etta pulled Felix around the corner of the laboratory table. Crouching behind it, she searched for any sign of stirring tangles, but all was still, for now at least. Marin drifted down to curl up in one of the chairs, her head resting on her arm as she murmured to herself.

Aside from Marin, the room was quiet.

'Could we have some reinforcements, please,' Etta hissed towards the half-open doorway. The smallest of her jumping spiders, barely the size of a kitten, waved a leg around the door. They took a tentative step in, then a few more as they were unceremoniously nudged the rest of the way by the others. They shuffled in sheepishly and huddled near the door.

Etta sighed.

'The wolfs might have been a better idea today.'

Felix peeped over the desk.

'Nothing's happening. Perhaps it's like the voices in my bedroom, it's just memories.'

Felix stood and took a step around the desk. He looked back at Etta.

'You are coming, aren't you?'

She nodded and beckoned the spiders over. A large black one with brilliant-coloured spots jumped onto the table, the painting reflected in their enormous eyes. The others fanned out behind Etta and Felix.

Felix examined the painting, while Etta monitored the room for furtive, tangle-like movements. Marin still seemed relaxed, almost sleepy, curled in her armchair. There were no signs of tangle webs in here, in fact the room had no cobwebs at all.

'Etta?' whispered Felix, standing on the chair now.

'What is it?' she asked, stepping up beside him.

'Look,' he breathed, pointing at the top corner of the frame.

Etta looked closely and saw the slenderest filament of silk, with a pearly ochre cast to it, hanging from the surface of the canvas like a loose thread. She squinted at it.

'That seems an unusual colour for spidersilk.'

Felix nodded. 'That's what I thought . . .' He lightly pulled at the silk, rotating his index finger slowly in the air, winding the silk like he did his mother's cottons.

'Look!' he exclaimed quietly, staring at his finger in amazement.

Etta looked, and then looked again, closer. Felix's finger seemed to be shimmering now.

'It's not going to fall off, is it?' she asked anxiously. 'I'll get in terrible trouble with Grandmother if I take you to her with bits missing.'

Felix was looking closely at the silk. 'Do you think it's the same colour as the background of the painting?' he asked Etta, the thread so long now he had to step off the chair.

Etta looked closer. As Felix twined the silk around his fingers, she saw the surface of the painting twitch in a way that was familiar, though she couldn't place where from.

'Knitting!' she suddenly cried.

The spiders and Felix all flinched.

'Sorry!' Etta whispered, holding up her hands apologetically. 'It just came to me.' She leaned her head against the wall to look across the surface of the painting. 'It's like when Grandmother is unravelling her knitting, those twitchy little jerky movements. Did spiders cover the painting in woven silk?'

'Can you knit with spidersilk?' asked Felix, surprised.

Etta nodded.

'We sew with it. The thread is really strong and because of the magic in the webs you can command it not to break, or to be waterproof or something.'

Felix already had a little ball of the silk in his hands and was winding it as he unravelled.

'There's no cobwebs anywhere else in this room though,' he noticed. 'How do you think it happened?'

'Perhaps Benita asked her spiders to spin a silk cloth onto her self-portrait? I just can't think what for.'

At that moment, the twitching, jerking motions reached

Benita's mouth, and the finger that gently rested against her lips began to disappear.

Etta gasped and Felix dropped the ball of silk in shock.

'What's happening?' he demanded.

Etta squared her shoulders and lightly touched her great-great grandmother's face. She could just feel the faintest change in texture where the silk lay over the canvas. If she hadn't watched Felix unravel it, she never would have known it was there.

'It's a glamour. Benita wove a false painting over the true painting, to hide something . . .'

Abruptly making the decision, Etta tore the silk away from the canvas. Benita's hand disappeared, and the painting beneath was revealed.

As Etta tugged the last scraps away, the blue tarantula on Benita's lap trembled again. Felix saw it too, and he took a fearful step back.

'Etta?'

'It's alright, Felix.'

'Etta, what if it's like the tangles? What if it attacks?' Felix's voice was high, and a little shaky.

'I don't think so. Look at the way she's holding it in the real painting.'

Beneath the glamour, the painted Benita hadn't caged the tarantula with her fingers but had her hands resting on her lap, the spider sat comfortably in her palm.

Etta put a foot on the armrest, leaning closer to the tarantula. It was large, but large in the normal sense, not in the Stitchwort sense.

'So, back then our spiders were normal?' she asked quietly.

'It's remarkably real, she was a very talented painter.'

Etta reached out again and ran a finger across the paint, marvelling at the tiny hairs and exceptional detail. Again, the spider trembled, a leg twitched, then stretched. It moved sideways across the canvas, as though it were on one of the moving silver screens Felix talked about. Then the leg pushed and came out of the canvas, away from it, appearing as a real spider leg in the real world. It groped around for something to rest on, so Etta quickly put her hand out.

'Is that wise?' hissed Felix.

Slowly, sleepily, the spider crept out of the canvas to rest on Etta's outstretched hands. Etta stared at Felix, her eyes wide in wonder, unaware of the way she mirrored Benita's position in the painting behind her.

'What on earth?' she breathed.

The spider nuzzled up against her thumb, then slowly started to clean itself.

'I think she's been in a torpor,' Etta whispered to Felix as she carefully lowered herself into the chair. 'A sort of hibernation.'

'For how long?' he wondered, crouching down to warily examine the beautiful tarantula. Her marks were almost like petals on a delicate china plate.

'I've never seen colouration like this before,' breathed Etta.

Thoroughly clean, the spider began to spin a gleaming thread from her spinnerets. Etta's eyes unfocused dreamily for a moment, as she sank into a connection with the spider. She concentrated on the vibrations that buzzed in her mind, translating the spider's sounds for Felix.

'She wants you to take it,' she whispered to Felix.

'Me? Why?' he gulped, looking apprehensively at the silk.

Etta's expression was awestruck. She looked up at the portrait of their great-great-grandmother.

'She was Benita's favourite; they were very close. Like a familiar. She says we have Benita's powers, but split between us. You're . . .' she laughed. 'She says you're a weaver, Felix, and I'm a wanderer. You work with the silk and I work with the spiders. She says Benita could do both, but our powers are stronger.'

Felix gaped at her.

'Stronger? How so?'

Etta concentrated on what the spider was telling her, making sure she had the meaning clear.

'Because the power is in two vessels, not mixed up in one. You can fully develop your silk-weaving skill, and I can fully embrace my ability to wander through the spiders. We can each concentrate on one aspect. But when we work together, she says we'll be even more powerful.' Etta grinned at Felix. 'We're a team!'

Felix held out a hand beneath the tarantula and her silk spooled onto it, coiling around his palm and forming a neat circle. When she finished, she broke the thread, then drew her legs close against her body, holding herself tightly.

'Oh no,' breathed Etta. She stroked the spider's back. 'Poor girl. If you hold on, we'll take you to my grandmother. She . . .' Etta's eyes clouded again, then filled with tears. 'She says it's her time, she was left here to wait for someone like Benita.' Etta held a hand out to Felix. 'She wants us to hold her.'

They sat, their tears trickling steadily, while Etta cradled the tarantula in her lap and Felix gently stroked her back. The spider's legs curled underneath her, and she stilled.

Eventually, Etta spoke.

'Let's put her on the desk for now,' she said quietly, clearing a space in the dust for the spider. The jumping spiders moved forwards and gently nuzzled Etta, then made a circle guarding the tarantula's body.

Felix held out the coil of silk.

'What do you think this is? I can hear it talking.'

Etta rubbed her nose and screwed up her face.

'*We* know the spiderwebs can catch ghosts but I'm not sure Benita knew that – she lived here before the curse began. We also know they can record dreams, and memories. Benita must have known that and left behind some memories. I think this could be message from her!'

'Like a recording?' Felix asked.

'You mean like on a gramophone?' Etta nodded. 'I think so.' She held out her hand. 'In the attic, it only worked when we both touched it. I think it needs both of our powers.'

Felix groaned, but he took the coil of silk and held it open, like a bracelet. They slipped their hands through from each side and clasped one another's wrists, the silk circling them both.

The threads twitched, then tightened, and the room spun around them.

Etta's stomach lurched and she felt as though she were falling. She put a hand out to steady herself, and found Felix's shoulder. Around them, the study was changing; now brilliant sunlight poured in through the windows. The brocade drapes shone a deep rose pink, the velvet armchairs glistened a rich purple. The plants were glossy and vibrant, bright exotic flowers tumbling from them, filling the room with colour and perfume. The brass instruments gleamed, bubbles rolled through the glass tubes and steam billowed. Etta and Felix turned together, seeing the books neatly lined up on the shelves, and the desk covered in sketches and paints.

Sitting at the desk was a smiling, blue-eyed version of Etta.

'Hello,' she said.

CHAPTER 25

FELIX'S FINGERS DUG INTO ETTA'S WRIST painfully.

'Er . . . hello?' Etta replied, thankful for the desk between them.

'I'm Benita Starling,' the girl continued.

'I, er, we know,' said Etta. 'I'm Etta and this is Felix.'

'For you to have found me, you must be like me,' Benita said. She seemed almost a little bit vacant, or like she was reading from a script.

'Er, yes, we both are. Sort of,' mumbled Etta. Benita wasn't translucent, like Marin, she looked as real as Etta and Felix. But something was off about the way she spoke.

'The real Benita has gone,' Benita continued.

'The real Benita?' Felix asked, confused.

'She has left me behind, to answer your questions.'

'Felix, I can't feel my spiders,' Etta whispered. 'I think we're inside the memory somehow.'

'Like Aerwynna's bubble?' asked Felix. 'We're in here, with

that.' He pointed at Benita. 'And the real world's outside?'

'What are you?' Etta asked Benita. 'Are you a ghost?'

Benita hadn't blinked or moved at all. She was as still as a statue, smiling the same smile.

'I'm a part of Benita Starling. I'm made of the memories she left behind in case any of her descendants ever came back here. She wanted you to know the truth.'

Etta leaned forward eagerly, her hand on the desk.

'Benita Starling, did you kill Edgar Starling?'

'Opening with that?!' gulped Felix, looking very alarmed. 'What if you make it angry?'

'I did not kill Edgar,' Benita replied calmly.

'What happened to Marin's sealskin?' asked Felix tentatively. 'Were you her friend? Did you kill her and take it?'

'Marin was my friend,' Benita said. 'I was studying rock pool ecosystems when we first met. She was afraid of me to begin with, but we eventually became friends. Marin introduced me to many selkies, and the merfolk. I learnt so much from them over the years. Through them I met other fae. We exchanged knowledge and ideas.'

Benita dropped her eyes, and her expression became regretful.

'Edgar usually ignored me, but he began paying attention. He started reading my research, asking questions. I was delighted to share everything; I thought my brother and I would finally have the close relationship I'd always dreamt of. But he began to take my papers and write up my work as his own. He was paid to publish articles, show 'his' drawings and speak at events. The money and status gave him greater access to high society, to fine things.' Benita sighed. 'He did not seek knowledge for the joy of it, only for what status it brought him.'

'This was after your parents had passed away?' Felix asked gently.

Benita nodded.

'Edgar controlled the staff, the finances, and kept me hidden away for years. He didn't want me to have friends or get married. If I did, he'd be found out and he'd lose access to my work.'

'You were lonely,' commiserated Etta. 'Kept isolated and alone, so you wouldn't have anyone to help you.'

Benita nodded again.

'I did have friends though. Edgar sees the fae as lesser creatures. He never experienced their music, their art and craftsmanship, their dancing, their feasts. He knows nothing of the incredible, fantastic worlds they'll share, if one proves themselves worthy. They gave me gifts and invited me to ever more secret parts of their culture and society.'

Benita stood and walked across the study to the bookcase. She moved some books and showed them the back of the shelf.

'I had to hide my gifts, my treasures, so Edgar wouldn't sell them to fund his lifestyle.' A small tarantula with pink speckles was tucked away at the back of the shelf. They guarded another glamour, an illusion, like the surface of the painting. Behind were magnificent shells, delicate jewellery and glittering potion bottles.

'How did you do this?' Etta asked. 'How did you make these hiding spaces?'

'The spiders are able to spin a pocket of sorts, and hide it behind a glamour,' she explained.

'A world within a world,' wondered Felix. 'The two overlap the same space.' He turned to Etta. 'Like when you and Marin were both trapped in the net, and she was inside you.'

Etta shuddered.

Felix looked at the back of the shelf.

'Edgar found your hiding places?' he asked.

Benita nodded.

'He locked my bedroom door while I was sleeping and ransacked my study.'

She held up a hand and Etta saw she was made of glimmering silk filaments. Benita splayed her fingers, stretching webs out between them. A remembered version of the study door opened, and a tall man entered. He had shoulder-length dark hair, and he would have been handsome were it not for his arrogant expression. He headed straight for the desk and began to rifle through Benita's drawers.

Benita watched sadly.

'Marin was visiting me the next morning. She was in the habit of bringing her sealskin to the house by then.' Benita looked at the two velvet armchairs side by side. 'She'd put it under her chair while we had tea and cake.'

Benita walked across and sat in the chair opposite the one Marin was settled in in their time. She selected another silk strand and peeled it off her dress. Holding it taut between her fingers she nodded her head towards the open door. Turning, Etta and Felix saw Marin enter and walk cheerfully almost halfway into the room, her sealskin bundle cradled carefully in her arms. As Marin saw the scattered books and papers on the floor her smile faltered.

Edgar Starling loomed behind the selkie girl's shoulder, cutting off her escape route. Marin turned and stepped back when she found Edgar close behind her. He grasped the pelt in her arms as she clutched it tighter. Edgar's brows lowered and his mouth twisted in fury as they grappled, loosening the folds of the sealskin in their struggle. Edgar blinked in surprise as the light from a large jewel hidden within played over his face. He shoved Marin back against the workbench and reached past her for Benita's instruments.

Etta looked away.

'That was the day that Marin was bringing me something very special, from the mer. A magical pearl they used to enhance their powers. I had been granted one tide to study it before Marin would return it to the sea.'

'If you were locked in your room . . . ?' Felix let the question hover.

'The spiders,' Etta answered for Benita. 'She saw it all through the eyes of her spiders.'

Benita nodded. She held up another strand of silk. 'Would you like to see more?'

'No!' interrupted Etta quickly. 'No thank you, we've seen enough.'

'I tried to stop him,' Benita continued. 'I tried to help, but he crushed many of my spiders. The ones who were left, I ordered to retreat to my tower. I hid the youngest and smallest, and asked the bigger ones to spin a rope so I could climb out of the window.'

'Edgar took Marin's sealskin and the Mermaid's Eye,' Etta stated.

Benita nodded.

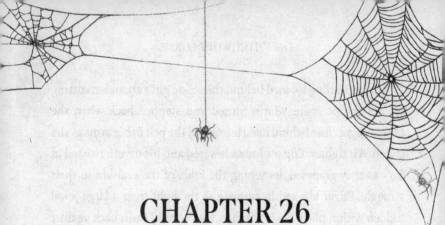

CHAPTER 26

'**D**O YOU KNOW WHERE THEY ARE NOW?' ASKED
Felix eagerly.

'No,' Benita replied sadly. 'I don't know what
happened to the Eye, or Marin's sealskin. After I escaped my room
I ran straight back into the house, terrified for Marin and furious
at what Edgar had done.'

Benita lowered her head, her expression chagrined.

'That's when I discovered my brother's secret experiment.
He'd been raising his own spiders, feeding them with dark magic.
He didn't have any magical talents of his own; it always rankled
him that he had no abilities. It's not uncommon in our family, we're
as likely to be an artist or scientist as a witch, but he wanted magic
and he always griped that it was wasted on me. In his jealousy and
entitlement, he took it.'

'What?' exclaimed Etta. 'How?!'

'His spiders. If they bite you, they can spin your gifts right out
of you. I'd noticed days prior that one of our garden boys was
missing – I assumed he'd left, or Edgar had fired him. One of

the stableboys had vanished a few weeks earlier too. I now think Edgar might have practised on them, because his spiders made short work of me. I was caught off-guard, and within moments I was powerless.'

Etta clutched at her throat: the thought that the tangles could have severed her connection with her spiders chilled her to her bones.

'Then what?' begged Felix, completely swept up in Benita's story.

'There was a terrible commotion.' Benita sat back in her favourite chair. 'Edgar didn't know what the Eye was, he just thought it was a magnificent pearl. The tide was turning, the mer had grown nervous. They sent Marin's brother to see what was happening and,' Benita looked down at her hands, 'he met one of the fae knights in the woods near my tower.'

Etta narrowed her eyes shrewdly. 'A fae knight loitering near your tower?'

Benita nodded.

Etta laughed.

'What?' asked Felix. 'What's happening?'

Etta snorted. 'Edgar was so busy keeping Benita away from humans, he didn't think about her going to balls and feasts under the hill with pretty fae courtiers!'

Benita nodded.

'Edgar thinks of the fae as lesser, as animalistic. Not as beautiful, intelligent, sophisticated . . .' A sly smile tugged at the corner of her mouth, small but there. 'I'd danced with all the fine fae of the court, but one in particular had caught my eye. There was nothing for me at home, so . . .'

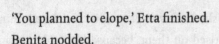

ALEXANDRA DAWE

'You planned to elope,' Etta finished.

Benita nodded.

'I'd been quietly packing my things and smuggling them out of the house. I was going to live with the fae – free of my brother, free to continue my research in peace with a loving partner who supported me and my interests.' Benita sighed, letting another gleaming strand of silk fall from her fingers.

'What happened?' asked Felix breathlessly. 'When the selkie and the knight came into the house? They found Edgar attacking you?'

Benita nodded. She looked around at the beautiful room she'd spent so much of her life in.

'Edgar's spiders warned him of intruders. He had their lines all over the house to pick up vibrations, to spy on the servants in case they were stealing.'

Etta frowned, noticing the study wasn't as bright now. The colours had faded, as though the sun had gone behind a cloud. She glanced down at the floor around Benita's feet, scattered with the dull threads she'd dropped, the memories taken from them, leaving the silk brittle and used up.

Benita stretched more webs between her fingers, faint images flickering across them.

'Edgar threw Marin's sealskin and the Eye into his study. He locked my door. Besides ourselves, only Marin knew where our rooms were hidden. He dragged me to his parlour, wrapped in aciniform silk.'

Felix looked at Etta.

'Wrapping silk, for binding prey,' she whispered.

188

'As I struggled, I could see Edgar running in and out of his study in a frenzy of activity; he wouldn't have considered Marin's family would send anyone so quickly. I don't believe he expected anyone to come looking for me either – he didn't think I had anyone.' She grinned fiercely. 'But I did! My love burst in, and their armour gave them a good defence against Edgar's spiders. Marin's brother helped me. I told him what was happening, and he ran for reinforcements.'

Etta blew out a breath sharply.

'Family legend says the house was attacked by fae, and that's how the east wing was destroyed.'

Benita nodded, letting more silk fall and drawing more out, surrounding them with tiny flitting shapes.

'The first fae to arrive were the simple garden creatures, but the word soon spread. These little ones battered the windows, threw stones. They managed to break in and swarmed around like bees. As more joined the fray, they began to overwhelm Edgar's spiders. He hadn't had time to fortify Stitchwort yet. If we hadn't had the Eye, it could have been the next day before Marin's brother came looking for her as she would sometimes sleep over. Edgar would have won easily.'

Felix squeezed Etta's hand and subtly inclined his head, indicating the room around them. It was faded now, with holes back to the real study beginning to appear and grow.

'Go on,' he urged Benita.

Benita sighed.

'I'm not sure of everything that happened. Edgar did something with his remaining spiders; they ran all over the walls, spinning a black thread. It almost seemed to sink into the walls, and if a fae touched it they were pulled in with it, screaming. I'd never seen anything like it – those filaments seemed spun from shadows, they were pure darkness. The fae tried to retreat, but the spiders hunted them down.'

'What about your spiders?' Etta asked.

'Many of them had already fallen.' Benita looked deeply sad. 'And I no longer had any powers to command them. More fae knights burst into the room and I heard my love shout for them to get me to safety. I was bundled from the parlour and once more locked in my tower.' Benita's eyebrow twitched, the only indication of her annoyance.

'I heard the clattering of hooves on the stairs and felt the tide must be turning against Edgar. This was my chance to escape this life.'

Benita smiled up at the self-portrait on the wall.

'Some of my spiders hatched in my crib when I was just a babe, they'd been at my side my entire life. I didn't need my powers to communicate with them. I asked them to spin out my memories of this dreadful day and hide them – hide them in a way only one with my powers would ever discover. Copying Edgar's spiders, they were able to spin out the memories, but I hadn't anticipated what it would do to me.'

'What do you mean?' asked Etta hurriedly. The past study had disappeared entirely now, leaving only Benita herself standing in front of them. Her eyes were shiny with tears.

'Without my memories of the day, I was confused. I didn't know what Edgar's spiders were or why an army of fae knights

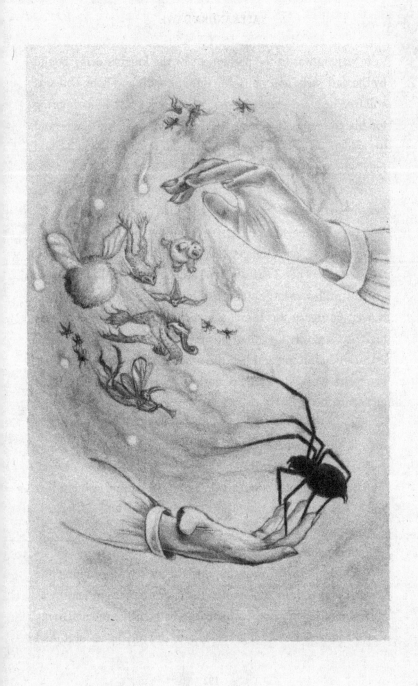

were waging war in the parlour. I saw the knights being bound by the dark webs and vanishing into the walls and floor. One was still free, he grabbed me and dragged me away with him, shouting for his comrades to retreat. He begged me to bind Edgar and his spiders inside Stitchwort, but without my powers, what could I do?'

Benita's tears fell as silk threads, falling and tumbling down her woven skin.

'He pulled me down the stairs, and I saw the remains of battle all around. Broken cabinets, fallen fae, a dryad struck down on the stairs . . . Then I saw the key – the key for the front door of Stitchwort. It was large and ornate, and Edgar had always lorded it over me that it was his. Our home and estate, everything was his. The key was a symbol of his power. All my memories of Edgar undermining and belittling me, of taking my work, those memories were still there. A flash of inspiration hit me, and I picked up the key.'

Benita stood straight and smoothed her skirts down, even as the silk unravelled and scattered on the floor around her.

'If he liked Stitchwort so much, he could rot in it,' she announced defiantly. 'I put the key in the door and swore Edgar and his spiders would never leave, as long as that door was locked.'

'But how, when you had no powers?' asked Felix.

Benita smiled knowingly.

'I'd lost my spider magic but I'm still a witch, from a long line of witches. I've read and studied the craft extensively, and I was born and raised in a house which drips with enchantments. In my fury, I connected to all of Stitchwort, to the very bones of it. As I turned that key, I felt the house shiver and I knew it had worked. Edgar would never leave.'

'Who set the house on fire?' Etta called. 'Quickly, there's not much time.'

Benita was fading, her silk disintegrating. She frowned.

'It wasn't on fire when I left.'

'What happened to your knight?' asked Felix quickly.

Benita smiled. 'I don't know. I am only made of memories before that day, not after.'

The last remnants of her broke apart and she faded.

Staring at the space where Benita had stood, Etta felt as though a cold hand had settled on the back of her neck.

'Felix,' she whispered. 'Felix, your mama unlocked that door . . .'

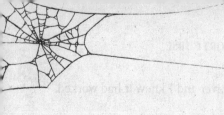

CHAPTER 27

THEY SAT IN THE HALLWAY, EATING. IT DIDN'T feel right to eat in Benita's study, not with her little tarantula still huddled on the table and knowing what had happened to Marin in there. Etta had propped the door open to allow some light into the corridor, and Marin still sat in her armchair, reliving happier times.

'We should find a happy memory of Benita and put it in the other chair for her to talk to,' suggested Etta.

Felix smiled faintly, then heaved a huge sigh.

'That was a lot to take in,' he said seriously.

Etta nodded.

'I'm sorry your great-great-uncle turned out to be a . . . a . . .' Felix groped for a word.

'Really terrible person?' Etta suggested glumly. She blew out a long breath.

'As far back as I remember, if I was scared, I'd think "What would Edgar do?" If I had a problem, I'd wonder how Edgar would solve it. He was my imaginary big brother, he knew everything, all the best games. He was kind and fun and,' she shook her head, 'totally, completely made-up.

'I had him wrong in every possible way. I thought Benita a rather dull character, if I thought of her at all. I thoroughly misjudged them both.'

Felix patted her knee and held out the last iced bun. 'If you don't mind a little brother instead of a big one, you've got me.'

Etta took the bun and broke it in half. She gave half back to Felix, then hugged him hard.

'Are you ready?' she asked, starting to pack up the picnic.

'Ready for what?' Felix asked.

'It's hours until dinner, and we know what we're looking for now.'

Etta laughed at Felix's blank expression.

'Benita's memory said Edgar threw the sealskin and the Eye into his study, and he had a secret door like hers. It must be along this corridor as well, it makes sense.'

Etta pointed one way.

'That's Benita's bedroom, in the bat tower,' she said, pointing behind them. 'And that . . .' She pointed the other way, to where the fire damage began. 'That's Edgar's parlour. I would assume his bedroom and other chambers were at that end of the house as well.' She put her hands on her hips and surveyed the hallway. 'Edgar's secret study door must be around here somewhere.'

Now that they knew what to look for, they quickly discovered the telltale hairline crack in the wall and a keyhole hidden in a knot in the dado rail. They made short work of trying the keys, until the door clicked and swung inwards with a groaning shriek.

The room beyond was a mirror of Benita's study – bookcases, a desk and a fireplace. Edgar's fireplace had only one chair, an imperious looking leather one.

'Like a throne,' snorted Felix.

It was much darker in here without Marin's light. They opened the drapes and lit another candle. Edgar didn't have experiments laid out on his table, he had stacks of glass tanks filling the centre. Plates were scattered everywhere, the shrivelled remains of meals dried on them. Cups overflowed with furry mould. Stained books were tossed haphazardly across the tabletop.

Etta held her candle close to a tank, examining the thick mass of white webbing spun across one corner.

'I think they're empty,' she said, relieved that no spiders had starved, trapped in captivity while the house lay empty.

Felix lurched violently back from a bigger tank, splashing candle wax on his hand.

'This one isn't!' he said shakily.

Etta cupped her hand against the glass to cut out the distracting reflections. She smiled.

'It's a moult, silly. A shed skin. It's big though. Edgar must have been breeding bigger and bigger spiders.'

'He truly was a monster,' muttered Felix with feeling.

Etta was examining the bookcase beside the window, with raised eyebrows.

'This is dark magic, really dark. I don't even know where you would get books like this!' She ran her finger along the titles. 'I can't even pronounce most of these words! I know "demonology", "grimoire" and "necromancy" but "inferna"? And what on earth is "goetic theurgy"?' She grimaced, wiping her fingers on her cardigan.

Felix joined her at the bookcase. 'Rites, hexes . . . Hexing doesn't sound too serious?'

'Well, it depends on who you're hexing, and why, and how good you are at it.'

Etta's finger lingered on the slightly sticky, black spine of *Mastering Hexes and Jinxes*. She shook her head and abruptly pulled her hand away.

'I think these books are dangerous.'

They both stood there for a moment, looking longingly at the dark spines of the books. Although there was something nauseating about them, they were also tempting, tantalising. Etta's fingers twitched towards them again.

'Ouch!' she cried, clapping a hand to her neck.

'Are you alright?' asked Felix, startled.

Etta held out her hand. One of her spiders, just the size of her thumbnail, was sat in her palm. She lifted her thick curls to show Felix her neck. There was a tiny red mark.

'They bit you?' gasped Felix, his eyes wide.

Etta gave the books a wary look and stepped back. She pulled Felix back with her. 'We should stay away from those books. It's definitely not safe. The last time a spider bit me I was about to step in a hornet's nest . . .' She shuddered.

They turned their backs on the alluring spellbooks and moved further into Edgar's study. A red crystal was nestled into a stand fashioned to look like a dragon's claw. It reminded Felix of the chickens' feet, and, laughing, he told Etta.

She stared at the crystal, her mouth open. 'Oh no . . .' she said weakly.

'What?'

'The crystals, Felix. The crystals we knocked over in the attic!' She put her hand over her mouth in horror.

'What about them?' Felix asked, unconcerned.

'*One of* them.' Etta looked stricken. 'Felix, one of them was huge and white and . . . and pearly! What if it was the Mermaid's Eye?'

'We gathered them all up again, so we know where it is!' Felix shouted joyously. He gave a jump and a whoop.

Etta was shaking her head.

'No, you don't understand. That one went off. It deliberately headed away from us. It went off deep into the attic, where we threw the eel webs. We'll have to search for it, without our parents finding out we went up there again!'

A glowing light appeared behind them and they both turned with guilty expressions, but it was just Marin. The ghost drifted into the room, rubbing her upper arms as though she felt cold.

'Marin!' Etta ran forwards to stop her. 'Marin, it isn't very nice in here, why don't you stay in Benita's room?'

You never see

Etta shivered as the ghost's voice slipped across her mind.

'I do see. I see that you were happier across the hall than in here. Go back, we'll come and get you when we're leaving.'

It's here

Felix joined them. 'Your sealskin? Can you feel it?' He gripped Etta's arm. 'He threw it in here and didn't have time to move it,' he hissed.

'Can you show us?' Etta asked gently, stepping aside to let Marin bob through.

The ghost floated slowly, shrinking back from the moth-eaten animal heads mounted on the walls. She didn't want to brush against anything in Edgar's room and cringed away from his possessions. Finally, she stopped, hovering by the fireplace in front of a heavily decorated picture frame surrounding a dark, mouldy canvas.

I can feel it

Her voice was gentle this time, wistful, and filled with longing; not as cold as usual.

Etta and Felix looked at each other.

'It can't be . . .' Felix began.

'He found her glamoured hiding places, and he'd stolen her spider magic,' Etta said, looking towards the open door and Benita's study. 'Maybe he stole one more of his sister's ideas.'

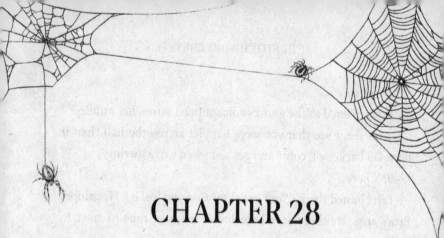

CHAPTER 28

THEY CLIMBED UP ON TO EDGAR'S LEATHER chair, it was more than big enough for two. The canvas and frame were filthy with grime and mildew.

'Let's lift it down,' suggested Etta.

With difficulty, they manoeuvred it upwards off the hook, but the ornate frame was heavy. As it came free of the fixings it overbalanced and fell face down onto the floor. Etta and Felix winced as it landed with a heavy, dull thud.

'Did anyone hear that?' whispered Felix.

Etta was frozen on the chair, darting through the minds of dozens of spiders, briefly borrowing their eyes as she flitted through the house.

'No, no one heard. We're safe.'

'Let's lean it up against the desk,' she said, gripping one side as Felix lifted the other. The painting rested against the wood, its darkened surface facing them. Marin came down close, her light illuminating heavy ridges and textures beneath the mould.

Felix peered closely. It wasn't a fungus, but the finest of

black silk threads woven together.

'Etta,' he whispered. 'It *is* the same as the other painting!'

Etta made a disgusted, exasperated sound.

'That man didn't have an original thought in his head! He always took the shortcut, stole Benita's work. He wanted all the credit, respect and money without working for it!' She folded her arms angrily. 'I'm not sure he's a Starling at all!'

Felix slowly stroked the surface of the painting, then shivered, pulling back his sleeve to show Etta the goosebumps. He ran his hand over the canvas again, and Etta thought she saw a sort of shimmer dance across the silk.

'I feel like something is here,' whispered Felix.

'Like Benita's study?' Etta asked. 'Or like the eels?' She hesitated. 'I'm not sure the memory of Edgar Starling is something we want to invoke; we don't know how much power these memories have. What if he can hurt us? The eels could.'

Felix shook his head.

'It's not like that,' he said quietly, as his fingers traced the black silk. When he'd almost reached the edge of the painting, Felix's finger seemed to snag on something.

'There!' he breathed. Very gently, as though afraid it would break, he pinched finger and thumb together, then began to slowly draw his hand away from the surface.

The silk was a thin sheet of black gossamer, so fine it became translucent when it stretched. Etta could make out part of a landscape through it, before the silk tore. As the hole widened, Etta took hold of the other edge and together they ripped the silk from the canvas, just as they had with Benita's painting.

'There he is,' Felix murmured as they stood before the painting. 'There's Edgar Starling.'

Marin recoiled savagely, flying up against the ceiling to get away.

Etta put her head on one side.

'Funny sort of painting, isn't it?' she asked Felix.

Edgar Starling was outside, near the cliff edge. The sea, the bay and the village beyond stretched out below him. He posed, lording it over his domain, a red cloak billowing around him.

Felix pointed at the signature in the bottom corner.

'Benita Starling painted this one as well,' he said.

Etta leaned in closely to look at the details. 'It does look like the same style as her self-portrait.' Her eyes narrowed as she touched upon the flowers in the painting.

'Tansy, petunia and sunflowers,' she murmured, before tracing along the cape Edgar was wearing, billowing gracelessly behind him. 'Felix, this seems strange.'

Felix crouched to look at where she was pointing.

'This cape isn't even blowing in the same direction as his hair. It looks clumsy. Benita couldn't have painted this. She was too careful, too meticulous to make such an error,' she said.

Felix poked the cape and shivered.

'When Edgar was trying to hide everything . . .'

'He must have done this,' Etta said. 'Edgar added the cape, badly. In a rush.'

They both stared at the heavy looking fabric, draped across Edgar's shoulders and straining towards the sea.

'Felix,' Etta whispered. 'I don't think it's just paint.'

Felix's eyes widened in understanding. Together they examined the edges of the painted cape. Etta tried to dig her nails in under. Felix crouched down and tried his hardest to prise the lower section away from the painting.

'Got it!' Felix exclaimed, as he pulled a slender black thread from the canvas. This time, as he unravelled, a section of the cloak began to fall away from the painted surface.

Etta held her hands out, catching the pelt as it was slowly released from the painting.

'It's definitely the sealskin,' she whispered to Felix. 'Look.' She showed him the black silk threads, how they passed through the skin and into the canvas. 'Remember, Benita said the tangles wove webs of pure darkness that sank into the

walls? I think they used those threads to make the sealskin part of the canvas.'

'Why bother to hide the skin inside the painting and then cover it with the black mildew glamour?' Felix wondered.

'Maybe in case anyone cleaned the mildew layer off, like we did?' Etta mused.

'Layer upon layer of secrets, lies and illusions,' Felix murmured.

Etta spread the skin out on the floor as best she could.

'It's messy with the paint, and it's got the dark silk woven through it as well. We'll need to remove that.' She sighed and looked up.

Marin was shivering in the corner of the room, up against the ceiling in an alcove.

'Marin? Marin, we've found it!' she called joyfully.

Marin tentatively peeked down, but her face was sorrowful.

No good . . .

She moaned.

'We'll clean it,' Etta promised. 'It'll be as good as new, I promise.'

'How are we going to do that?' asked Felix, poking at the cracked paint layer.

'We'll have to take it to my grandmother,' Etta replied. 'She's an expert in dealing with all manner of spillages. I've had glue in my hair, and Father fell in honey once, ended up with honey-covered bees in his beard. Mother had a terrible afternoon one summer with sticky sap and an ants' nest, she had bites and blistering skin and all kinds. Grandmother's the best at rescuing anything from stains and spills, she has all the potions.'

'How will we explain why we have a sealskin? And what about Marin?' Felix asked.

Etta carefully rolled the skin up and stood.

'I'm sure we can make it sound like we just found it by chance,' she said confidently. 'We can't keep Marin hidden forever, we've had a few close calls already. Shall we take it to her now? Then we can wash for dinner and help her get the potions on it this evening.'

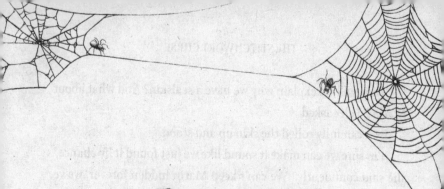

CHAPTER 29

ETTA QUIETLY TAPPED ON THE DOOR, THEN pushed it open.

'Grandmother?' she called, leading Felix to an elaborately carved couch, the cushioned seat and back of which looked distinctly nibbled. Marin floated off, exploring the cluttered rooms. Felix sat on the couch and Etta placed the rolled-up sealskin beside him.

'We'll wait a while, she's probably not gone too far.'

Etta took a few biscuits from her supplies bag and shared them with Felix. She sat in the chair opposite him, taking off her cardigan.

This room was far, far warmer than anywhere in the house, even the kitchen, and it smelt strongly of earth, mushrooms, forests and fur. The dank, dense air sat thick in her chest.

Etta held out her hands to warm in front of the fire and watched Felix as he looked around. On the chair beside hers was curled a sleeping rabbit, with soft, velvet ears laying flat along its back. The mantlepiece over the fire was entirely covered with mismatched teacups, each containing an old bird's nest, several with baby squirrels curled in them. There were luxuriant ferns everywhere, revelling in the moist humidity. In the alcoves either side of the fire were shelves. The upper ones were full of books and mounted animal skeletons. The lower shelves were lined with blankets and cushions. Felix pointed at a large sleeping animal on the bottom shelf closest to him.

'What's that?' he whispered.

'Badger,' mumbled Etta thickly around her biscuit. 'They don't do much in winter. Sleep quite a bit.'

'And what are they?' he asked, pointing to the shelf above the badger.

'"edge'og,' she managed, spraying crumbs into the fire.

'A what now?' he asked. All Felix could see was a jumble of what looked like thorns.

Etta finished her biscuit.

'Sorry, Father's biscuits are so good. The butter only melts on your tongue like this when he makes them. Those are hedgehogs, haven't you seen one before? They're hibernating. Are you eating your biscuit?' she asked hopefully.

Felix absently took a bite as he continued to stare. There was a barn owl on the chandelier above them, its head tucked under one wing in sleep.

'That's Gladys,' Etta told him. 'Grandmother healed her broken foot a few years ago and she's stayed ever since.'

The central drawer of a dresser behind him had been left open. It was full of water, moss and stones and a fat toad was gazing out at him from under some irises.

In the adjoining room, a door opened and Grandmother swept in holding a bunch of herbs, with a flurry of snow nipping at her ankles. She unbuttoned her black coat and hung it up as the snowflakes scattered across the arms and shoulders began to melt.

Patting her iron-grey bun, she strode into the workroom. Grandmother stopped abruptly when she saw Etta and Felix by the fire. She nodded and gave one of her fleeting smiles, tugging her gloves from each gnarled finger.

'Good afternoon, children,' she said, continuing to her worktable. Formerly a dining table, it had elegantly curved legs and matching chairs that would seat sixteen people. At the moment, it was just seating one rather subdued looking raven, perched on the back of a chair. Grandmother glanced sideways at the bird as she placed her gloves down on the once-glossy surface of the table, now scorched and damaged, littered with notebooks, bottles and surgical instruments. Behind her, a tangle of brass tubes and glass vessels bubbled, boiled, dripped and hissed, just like in Benita Starling's study. Clouds of fragrant steam escaped the equipment, coating the paintings above with dripping condensation. It was no wonder that the plants were thriving in this tropical atmosphere.

Grandmother picked up a pestle and mortar and began to pound the herbs. As the fresh, zesty smell reached her nose, Etta inhaled deeply and felt more awake.

'Have you been in the greenhouses?' she asked.

'Clearly,' replied Grandmother. 'And I saw your parents taking a stroll together, young man.'

'How is my papa?' Felix asked quickly.

'Stronger. More alert. Putting on weight nicely,' Grandmother replied crisply. 'There,' she said with finality as she finished pounding the herbs into a paste. She dipped an arthritic-looking mauve finger in and brought it up to her sharp eyes, nodded, and slowly added steaming water, stirring the paste into a thin gruel. She looked over at Etta and Felix.

'Is this a social call?'

Felix squirmed in his chair as her bright blue eyes fell on him. Etta cleared her throat.

'Actually, we, er, we found something and we'd like to show you,' she began. 'It's sort of an old fur, it's in a mess.'

Felix stood and picked up the sealskin. They brought it over to the table and unrolled it, fully revealing the mess of fur and paint.

As Grandmother came closer to examine it, Marin bobbed up without warning, causing her to stop abruptly. Grandmother surveyed the ghost coolly, then turned her sharp gaze onto the children.

Etta twisted her hands around one another.

'Also, we found a ghost.'

There was silence. Grandmother simply waited, one eyebrow arched high on her forehead.

'You see, it seems that ghosts can get trapped in the cobwebs sometimes, and we can't see them, but Felix can. So he started to unpick it and the next thing she was free, and . . .' Etta stopped babbling as Grandmother switched her searchlight glare onto Felix.

'I, er . . .' Felix began, hunching in on himself under her scrutiny. 'It was very scary, the cobwebs started talking to me and then she came out. She looked sad, like she needed help.'

Marin had retreated behind Etta, but she peeped up over Etta's shoulder and nodded her head rapidly.

Grandmother still had her piercing blue eyes fixed intently on Felix. She tapped her finger against her chin a few times, then opened a tin on the table.

'Here.' Grandmother offered them a scone each. 'These will help you feel better. James is baking extra fortitude into everything at the moment.' She smiled thinly, but it was kind.

Then she pinned her fearsome stare onto Marin.

'Anything to add, young lady?'

The ghost shrank back, disappearing inside a threadbare armchair, accidentally dislodging a snoozing goat with her icy elbow.

Grandmother turned back to Etta.

'You are aware of what manner of creature that is? And, therefore, of what this is?' she asked, her lips thin and white as she jabbed a long, plant-stained fingernail at the sealskin.

Etta nodded.

'I know you don't like the fae, but that's not her fault! She was trapped here against her will. She just wants to go back to her home, but she can't until her skin is restored and whole again. She can't help who she was born as,' Etta said stubbornly, meeting her grandmother's gaze.

'Well, we certainly don't want her sort here,' Grandmother grumbled. 'We want to be rid of her as quickly as possible, before she causes trouble.'

Etta folded her arms.

'You can't just decide you know what someone's like based on what they look like or where they're from.' She scowled. 'Marin's lovely, and she needs our help. Our family caused her death and took her sealskin away!'

Grandmother's other eyebrow climbed to join the first.

'We've discovered that Edgar Starling actually wasn't very nice,' Etta continued. 'He lied and stole. He probably caused the curse too. We found his study in the ruined wing, we discovered poor Marin! He stole her sealskin, he covered it in paint, *ruining* it, then he hid it and he *murdered* her!' She realised she was shouting and waving her arms about. Grandmother's face hadn't moved.

'And, um,' Etta quietened down, her ears burning, and shuffled to stand beside Felix, 'I think it's only honourable that we right the wrongs someone in our family did to Marin and her family. It's in our power to fix her sealskin and get her home.' She lifted her chin defiantly. 'And Felix and I are going to do it anyway, whether you help us or not. It's the right thing to do.'

'But we would like your help. Please,' added Felix nervously. Grandmother still hadn't said anything. 'You know all the potions and things that will help to clean the skin.'

Before Grandmother could speak, a voice came from behind them, dangerously low.

'You took my son into those collapsing ruins? When you were supposed to be looking after him, and keeping him safe?'

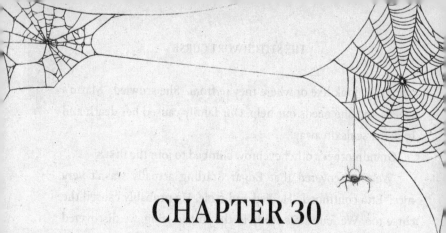

CHAPTER 30

VIOLA WAS ABSOLUTELY FURIOUS. SHE TOOK Felix's sleeve and pulled him out of the infirmary, down the hall, all the way to the kitchen steps. Etta could barely keep up with her marching. Sensing her anxiety, spiders started to gather along their route, pausing at the kitchen doorway beyond which only the wolf spiders were allowed, and even then, only at night.

'James!' Viola barked so loud that Father dropped his rolling pin on his foot and stood on one leg, a pained expression on his face.

'Are you aware of what the children have been doing? Running unsupervised around this deathtrap?'

Father rubbed at his beard, his brow furrowed as he looked over Etta and Felix.

'They appear to be intact, what's going on?' he asked in a bewildered tone.

The kitchen door shunted open and Mother shuffled in with two large buckets of vegetables. She placed them down and started to tug off her snow-covered boots before she saw Viola in the centre of the kitchen, her hands on her hips, and the children huddled together near the door.

'What's happened?' she asked quickly. 'Are they alright?'

'They,' Viola began, her voice vibrating with rage, 'have been running around playing in the ruined wing, where you swore they wouldn't go because it is so dangerous. Rotten floors, you said. Collapsing ceilings! They've been exploring it, finding secret rooms, murders, and talking to a . . . a ghost!' Viola's voice raised in pitch, high and shrill and piercing.

Mother's mouth fell open. 'Etta, you wouldn't!' she cried, aghast. 'You would never put your cousin in such danger.'

But Etta couldn't meet her mother's gaze, she looked down at the ground which was all blurry through her tears.

'Mama,' Felix said, stepping forwards. 'It's not Etta's fault, I wanted to . . .'

'We're safe here, *schatje*!' Viola interrupted. 'Safer than I ever thought we would be. Etta's never been out there, she can't understand . . . I've lived through one world war already, and an influenza pandemic, and now another war! The curse hides this house; we're invisible, we're safe. Your papa can get better, we can live here in secret, away from it all . . .'

The telling off went on for quite some time, until they were banished to their bedrooms with no dinner. As Etta and Felix trudged up the hall, they were accompanied by slow, drawn-out scratching noises.

'What is that?' gulped Felix, his eyes flitting around anxiously.

'Ivy,' Etta replied flatly. 'Mother's spreading the ivy out across the doors and windows so we can't climb out.'

A raven hopped along one of the hall tables, watching them

closely with bead-bright eyes. It cawed loudly, and was answered by a second, waiting on a branch for them to pass up the stairs. There were no spiders to be seen.

'What's happening?' Felix huddled closer to Etta, not liking the scrutiny of the birds.

'Grandmother,' Etta said dully. 'She's set the birds to watch us, to make sure we don't sneak around.'

'Where are your spiders?' Felix asked, checking the corners for the architects of the empty webs hanging there.

'Birds eat spiders, Felix. Even the biggest spiders are wary of them, especially the corvids. The little ones eat them too though; garden birds feed spiders to their young.'

The raven on the branch swooped down to land heavily in front of them, with another grating call. Felix's eyes widened as he took in the wingspan, the length of the talons and the size of its beak. The raven hopped up to them and began jabbing at the supplies bag Etta still had over her shoulder.

'Off!' she shouted, clasping the bag tight to her chest. The raven turned to Felix instead, flapping its huge wings and stabbing its sharp beak at his bag.

'What does it want?' cried Felix, ducking and weaving, trying to avoid the aggressive bird.

'Food! They always want food.' Etta held up a squashed bun. 'Here!' she called, and hurled it down the corridor, away from them both. 'Quick, run to your room and shut the door!' she advised as she started jogging to her tree.

'Goodnight!' shouted Felix, as he fled to safety of his own bedroom.

Etta wiped her eyes with her last dry handkerchief and sat up. She was all cried out now – her eyes were stinging, her throat raw and she had a throbbing headache. She felt nauseous with hunger, but her throat was too sore to eat anything. She sighed, leaning her head on the wall and closing her eyes.

This is all my fault. I was so excited to have an adventure, to find clues, lift this curse and change our lives. I didn't think about the danger I was putting Felix in, even after he nearly drowned.

She covered her face with her hands, the tears threatening to spill again.

It has been really, really dangerous. Why didn't I see that sooner?

But a tiny part of her still argued it had been worth the risk. They'd learned so much about the family curse. She felt so close to untangling it and finding their freedom.

In coming here, the Greys were trapped. They might not mind it now, with a war outside, but in time they'd run out of coffee, they'd miss their news on the wireless and shows on the silver screens. Soon it would be summer, and they'd be standing in the garden with a nettle tea, trying to find a spot with a view of the beach to watch the villagers having fun.

A burning resentment began to build. *What Felix and I were doing is good for everyone! We're helping people, like Marin, and getting the Eye back for the mer so they can protect their community, which benefits the whole area for humans as well! I won't be told off for doing the right thing.*

She scowled.

This is bigger than just what's easy and comfortable for us.

There came a light tapping at her window. Etta looked up to see an orb weaver, a round-bodied garden spider with markings like an oak leaf on its back.

Etta climbed along the tree's interior wall to reach the window. The glass was warped from decades of the beech pressing against it, and some of the panes were loose. Etta wiggled a cold piece of it free and the spider entered, slipping under the ivy and spinning a thick thread behind herself. She climbed up the window and began to spin a new web, spiralling round and round, filling the window frame.

'What's this for then?' asked Etta curiously, sitting on the window ledge.

'Etta?' asked Felix, his voice strangely distant.

She sat up, looking around.

'Felix? Where are you?'

'In my room. I thought we might be able to speak through the silk, using the vibrations. That's all sound waves are, vibrations.'

Etta beamed at the spiderweb.

'Felix! You connected with an orb weaver! That's wonderful!'

'I didn't exactly,' he explained. 'I saw them sitting on the ivy outside my

216

window and I asked if they'd spin a thread from me to you so we could talk. I wasn't sure they'd do it, or if it would work!'

Felix sighed deeply.

'I'm sorry, Etta. I'm sorry my mama overheard us talking and got so cross. She's not stopped worrying since the war started. She's so on edge, everything just makes her angry now. She's trying to keep everyone safe.'

'I know. But that's what we're doing as well,' Etta said. 'What about Marin and the mer? We're not safe until everyone is safe.'

'She said we must go straight to breakfast tomorrow, then straight to the library for extra lessons,' Felix said glumly. 'And we're only allowed in the kitchen, the library or our bedrooms.'

Etta nodded. 'Eat, sleep, school. Nothing else.'

'So . . .' Felix continued. 'That means we only have tonight.'

Etta leaned forwards, intently focused on the spiral web sparkling in the light of the waning moon.

'Only have tonight for what, Felix?'

'Going into the attic to find the Mermaid's Eye.'

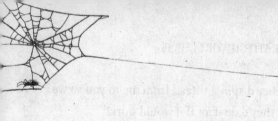

CHAPTER 31

THEY TIPTOED CAREFULLY THROUGH THE ATTIC, wary of any sounds that might wake the sleeping adults below. The candlelight guttered in the eddying draughts that swept by; it seemed the dancing shadows were reaching for them. As they edged around the crystal balls, glittering in their golden glow, a curl of darkness hung from the table. Etta's arm prickled, all the hairs standing on end as she remembered their encounter with the eels.

She shivered, thankful for Felix beside her, and pushed on into the darkest, most cluttered section of the attic. Etta felt as though her spiderlings were crawling all over the back of her neck, it itched uncomfortably. Standing back-to-back, Etta and Felix turned slowly in a circle, all of Etta's senses screaming that someone was there with them, but there were only gently fluttering shrouds of old spiderwebs, darkened with dirt.

'I'm so jumpy,' whispered Felix, holding his candle higher to see further ahead.

Something caught Etta's eye.

'Look!' she pointed at the floor, where a staggering line was visible in the thick dust. 'The Eye could have made that.'

Felix crouched down and examined where the path began, below the edge of the table.

'It's the only clue we have,' he agreed. 'We follow?'

Etta nodded decisively, and they moved stealthily onwards, sweeping the candles from side to side to check for any creeping dangers.

'Do you think there's tangles up here?' Felix asked shakily.

Etta shook her head.

'I don't think so, I'm not seeing their sort of webs.'

'But your spiders don't come up here,' Felix pointed out. 'They don't go in the ruins because of tangles. Maybe up here is the same?'

Etta squeezed his hand reassuringly.

'I'm positive there are no tangles up here. Maybe they can sense Harold's ghost, and the eels, and they don't like the . . . the . . . psychic vibrations or something.'

Felix smothered a laugh.

'You think ghosts give spiders headaches?'

Ignoring him, Etta pointed ahead to where the ceiling was highest. A thick column of brick chimneys soared up to the roof, surrounded by teetering heaps of dusty old junk.

'Look,' Etta said, her head on one side. 'Those black webs strewn about up there, do you think they're the ones we threw away?'

They cautiously moved closer, holding the candles up to the hammocks of webs. As they watched, a faint blue spark crackled from one cobweb to another.

'Definitely,' confirmed Felix.

'What a strange place,' Etta commented, bemused, as she looked around. There was a circle of floor that was mostly clear of dust and dirt, except for desiccated remains of things she didn't want to look at too closely. Everything was piled haphazardly up against the brick tower in the most random, gravity-defying manner. Of course, the trail they were following led right into the heart of the mess.

Felix groaned, craning his neck to look up at the piles of old furniture, boxes, ornaments and clothes.

'We have to search that whole trash heap tonight? It'll take hours!'

'We're going to struggle to stay awake in lessons tomorrow,' Etta said ruefully.

She moved forwards until she was standing in front of the mounds of clutter, crouched low, searching for the Eye, when above her head a perfect circle of junk flew open, like the lid of a gigantic saucepan. Six enormous striped legs lunged out to snatch at her.

Etta reflexively jerked back, her mouth agape as she stared up at the huge fangs bristling above her head. Instinctively she thrust her candle forwards into the jaws. The enormous spider squealed and thrashed, retreating rapidly into its lair.

Felix grabbed her under her arms and pulled her backwards out of range as the trapdoor slammed shut again.

Etta's ears rang in the silence, drowning out her racing heart and ragged breathing.

'That was the biggest spider I've ever seen in my life! Fast too,' she gasped. The whole encounter had been over in a few heartbeats.

Etta pushed herself up on to her hands and knees, glaring at the door to the spider's lair. The meandering trail stopped just beneath it.

'Felix, I think the Eye is in there. We have to go inside.'

'This is a terrible idea,' whispered Felix, standing in the fireplace looking up.

'It's an excellent idea,' retorted Etta from the bedroom doorway. Through the crack, she watched Gladys swoop down the corridor. Owls and corvids disliked each other intensely, so the barn owl was the perfect distraction to keep the ravens' prying eyes away from them. 'We can't very well go in through the trapdoor, right where the spider's waiting. We'll have to creep in another way. We should be right under her part of the attic here.'

'Are you positive there's a back way in?' Felix objected, ducking out under the mantlepiece.

'Yes, I told you!' Etta repeated. 'Some of these chimneys are storm damaged further up; the broken parts are open in the attic.'

Etta tugged hard on the silvery spidersilk rope she'd fastened the grappling hook to with a complicated knot.

She looped the silk around a large and particularly fluffy tarantula with deep-pink and black hair, and the spider steadily began to climb up the back of the fireplace, the grappling hook dangling at her side.

Felix leaned forwards to watch the spider's progress.

'Will she be alright, climbing up there?' he asked.

'Look at you,' Etta said joyfully. 'All worried about the spiders! Yes, she'll be fine – she's an arboreal species, a tree dweller, and therefore an excellent climber.' Etta slipped a bag over her shoulder and handed another to Felix. 'You'll be pleased to know wolf spiders aren't very good climbers, so you won't have to squash in close with any of them!'

Felix opened his bag and looked inside as Etta grasped the rope and braced a foot against the wall.

'Etta, this is empty.'

'I know.' She tilted her head to look back at him, her face upside down as she began to climb. 'It's to put the Eye in. As soon as one of us has it, start making your way back here.' She disappeared from view.

'Etta?' Felix stepped back into the fireplace, looking up into the chimney. Tiny lights glimmered where Etta had sent some of the smallest spiders to light the way for them. 'Etta, are you expecting it to chase us? I won't leave you behind.'

'Female trapdoor spiders never wander far from their lair,'

she called back quietly. 'Hurry up, *I'm* the one leaving *you* behind now!'

Etta had been right about where the damaged chimneys joined up in the attic, there was indeed an opening they could climb out of. Moving quietly, they perched on the edge of the hole in the brickwork, the shaft yawning open behind them.

'Look, Felix,' Etta breathed as loudly as she dared. The chimney column stood like a tent pole in the centre of the dark attic space. The junk formed an encircling perimeter wall ten feet away from them. Sheets of the spider's white webbing hung from the chimneys and swagged out to the junk piles, like a macabre big top. 'All of this is her lair!'

The spider's den was a maze of silk sheets stretched between the masonry of the house and piles of old furniture. Hammock-like webs swagged the space, remains of past meals littered the floor.

In the darkness, Etta could just make out the glitter of Felix's eyes as he slowly nodded in astonishment, the scale of the spider's nest becoming apparent.

'Is there any way of telling where she is?' asked Felix quietly. The curtains of silk were opaque grey sheets in the darkness, the attic relics creating shadowy corners and pockets where anything could be lurking.

'If we've come out where I think we have . . . she'll be on the other side of these chimneys, by the trapdoor, waiting for dinner,' reassured Etta, indicating for the tiny spiders to fan out and give them some light. 'As long as we don't make any vibrations, we'll be safe. She'll never even know we were here.'

'Are they safe?' Felix pointed at the smallest spiders as their lavender glow began to give shape to the maze surrounding them.

Etta smiled.

'They're far too small for her to bother with. She'll be much more interested in us!' she finished brightly, as she stepped out onto the attic floor.

It was slow, painfully slow. They crept around dusty furniture and ducked under hanging sheet webs, trying to avoid creaking floorboards and looking always for the Eye.

'Are you sure it's in here?' asked Felix for the third time.

Wordlessly, Etta pointed at the faintest of white glows to their left and flashed a triumphant grin.

'Hopefully she's far enough away that she won't pick up our vibrations,' Etta whispered. 'With a bit of luck, we can just scoop it up and we'll be back in bed with no one any the wiser.'

'There was a lot of "with luck" and "hopefully" in that speech,' muttered Felix.

Creeping and hunched, Etta and Felix slowly crawled from one hiding place to the next, steadily making their way to an area of broken floorboards beneath a thick layer of webs, where a glowing white ball had fallen and now rested, trapped in the framework of floor joists.

'Be careful!' hissed Felix, grabbing Etta's ankle in alarm as she braced herself over the floor void and began shuffling under the webs.

Etta soothed him. 'She's old, and it's cold up here. I'm sure she's snuggled down, all warm and sleepy in her nest for a nice, long nap. You keep watch, I'll get the Eye and we'll sneak back out.'

Etta took a deep breath, hoping she'd convinced Felix of her confidence. The spider was old, which meant she was probably quite cunning, as well as having formidable size and speed.

And she has the advantage of this being her territory. The sooner we're out of here the better, Etta thought grimly as she began to crawl forwards. She reached the first of the thick, trailing cobwebs and slid easily between them.

Etta couldn't see or hear Felix now. All sound except for her own shallow breathing was muffled by the gauzy hangings all around her. It was like being gently smothered by a cloud; she could see and hear nothing beyond her own hands.

She paused, peering through the hanging trails of old webs. Just visible ahead was the softly gleaming light. The huge pearl rested at the base of a thick wooden post. As Etta squinted through the dust, she saw it move slightly, as if trying to roll away, but it had fallen into a gap and become trapped.

Etta raised herself on to her hands and knees to shuffle forward some more. She wasn't close enough to reach out for it yet. Etta resisted the urge to lunge and grab it, to get out of this awful mess.

It smells terrible!

The torn and broken bodies of the spider's prey littered the floor all around her. Etta put her knee down on a tiny, sharp bone and gasped at the pain, biting the inside of her cheek so she wouldn't cry out. She inwardly groaned when she noticed the fresh remains of a large black bird, a rook or crow, tangled in the webs ahead. If that fell on her . . . She grimaced.

This really is most unpleasant!

Etta was close enough now to reach out, her fingertips stroked the glistening white ball, pulling silk threads away from it. It gleamed with a warm lustrous light. It was warmer than the floor beneath her, smooth and tactile. She tried to wriggle her hand underneath it, to silently lift it from its trap. It wobbled, then she managed to grasp at it and jerk the ball towards her. She triumphantly curled her hand around it and started to wriggle backwards, keeping an eye on where the nearby webs began to spiral towards a debris-strewn hole.

Etta nearly screamed in shock as she bumped into something behind her, something warm and soft.

Felix swiftly covered her mouth with one hand and pointed, eyes wide, to the top of the curtains of thick cobwebs.

'Shhhh,' he hissed urgently.

Something was moving in there.

CHAPTER 32

THE TRAPDOOR SPIDER WAS EASILY THE biggest Etta had ever seen. It was far, far bigger than the pumpkin-sized giants in the greenhouses. It could effortlessly eat one of the chickens. Etta thought it could possibly eat her and Felix.

They had drawn back into the shadows, the tiny spiders in Etta's hair dimming their lights. They watched as the behemoth fussed around with the webs, its long, thick legs stroking and smoothing the edges of the nest, discarding mummified bats and mice that were stuck in the hanging veils, throwing them to join the bones of small mammals that littered the floor.

As the spider performed her housekeeping, she steadily drew closer to them. She was in between them and the chimney they'd climbed up from the bedroom.

Etta looked at the opening in the webs that could only lead to the trapdoor the spider had attacked her from earlier. *If we go out that way, we'll be straight out into the attic. That's much quicker than abseiling down the chimney.*

She pointed to the tunnel and began crawling. Felix frantically clung to her clothes to hold her back, shaking his head, his lips pressed together.

Etta stilled as movement caught her eye. *Was there something? There, in the shadows.* She stared intently, not even blinking, for five rapid heartbeats. Then she saw it, a great, striped leg silently gliding downwards.

She shuddered. The spider's paws were bigger than her fist. Its legs were the size of Etta's where they joined with its patterned abdomen. Etta nodded to Felix to look, and his eyes grew wide with horror as the spider began to patch up the webs they'd just crawled through.

Etta put her mouth close to Felix's ear.

'We can't go that way, we'll trigger the new webs. The only way out is through the trapdoor.'

As they reached the tunnel opening, Etta silently moved the Eye to Felix's bag, and indicated for him to go first. He shook his head furiously.

Glancing behind to see where the spider was, Etta risked whispering again.

'Felix, you take the Eye, you have to get it back to the mer. If she follows, maybe I can make a connection with her and slow her down. I'll be right behind you, I promise.'

Etta boosted Felix into the tunnel. He immediately turned and offered his hand to pull her up.

Etta froze as a dark shadow passed over her. A thick leg touched down at the side of her head, then another by her opposite elbow. Etta didn't dare move or breathe. She could tell the spider was searching the webs above from the way the cobwebs swayed rhythmically in time with the beast's movements.

Then Etta felt a pressure on her shoulder, and she went cold and sick. One of the spider's feet was resting on her.

She was effectively pinned to the spot. If she tried to move it would feel her. Would it sense her heat? Taste her?

She was sweating now, but there were layers of nightclothes and jumpers between her sweat and the spider's senses. Would that keep her hidden? Etta was almost crying in terror, desperate to take a breath but too afraid.

Felix crouched just inside the tunnel, his eyes locked on the leg that pinned Etta in place.

'GO,' she mouthed at him.

With tears in his eyes, Felix shuffled backwards, not making a sound.

Etta stayed as still as she could, her eyes closed and her heart hammering so hard she thought it would burst. The spider lowered another leg, not to rest on Etta this time, but to lightly pat up her arm, to her hair . . . *as soon as she touches my skin, she'll sense my body heat, my sweat* . . . Etta could hear the spider's mouthparts smacking wetly in anticipation of the unexpected feast, the claws clicking as they moved.

Something came flying out of the tunnel, sailing over Etta's shoulder, tearing through the webs and hitting the floor with a doughy thud. The spider took off after it, moving with a speed Etta wouldn't have believed possible. Another missile whizzed by, but Etta didn't turn to look, she launched herself into the tunnel and began frantically crawling up it, coming nose to nose with Felix.

'What are you doing?!' she hissed loudly. 'You're going the wrong way!'

'Did it work? Did I distract her?' Felix was already turning around and heading up the silken passage.

'Yes! Thank you!' Etta said to the soles of Felix's boots as they tore along the passage. 'What did you throw?' asked Etta curiously.

'I'm not sure,' Felix's voice floated back to her. 'I think one used to be a rat. I'd very much like to have a bath and never think about it again!'

The whole tunnel suddenly lurched, then begin rhythmically swaying.

'Faster, Felix,' Etta cried. 'She's found us!'

Ahead, Felix reached the top, he shoved the trapdoor open and fell out into the attic, scrabbling at the furniture pile for anything he could use to defend himself.

Etta risked a glance over her shoulder and saw the spider's head and front legs filling the tunnel as she bore down upon them. Crying out, Etta flung herself out of the trapdoor as well. As she scrambled to her feet, wrenching a chair from the pile, the spider lunged at her, only to be hit over the head with a lamp Felix was holding.

The lamp barely slowed her for a second before she was on Etta. The spider's shiny, curved claws scrabbled at Etta's arms, catching in the wool of her cardigan. The hairs on the spider's legs and paws were thick, like wire bristles, scratching painfully at Etta's hands as the creature tried to get a grip and haul her into the lair.

Etta met the largest pair of liquid black eyes in the centre, and she tried to make a connection. For a fraction of a second, she saw herself through the spider's eyes, then she pushed too hard and broke the contact.

The spider reared up and back, a move that Etta knew came just before the downward strike that would see her as tomorrow's breakfast. Etta swung the chair up and drove it as hard as she could

towards the spider's face. The creature's head was so wide the chair legs wedged on either side of it, trapping the spider's scarlet fangs behind the seat.

Felix threw the lamp as he and Etta began rapidly retreating, stumbling over their own feet as they backed away. Pulling the chair from her face with her feelers, the spider lunged at them again.

'She won't leave her tunnel,' Etta said. 'Females rarely leave the tunnel, we're safe.'

Taking another step, the spider left the tunnel and began advancing across the floor towards them.

'Throw anything!' cried Etta, hurling an old vase. 'Just keep retreating, she'll return to her nest eventually!'

Felix didn't answer, he just lobbed a leather case with grim determination.

The spider kept advancing, dodging missiles with the same speed and agility with which she snared prey from behind her trapdoor. Etta and Felix had to keep checking over their shoulders to make sure they weren't backing themselves into a corner, and the spider took every opportunity to advance when they weren't looking. It had six eyes; five glittered like Grandmother's jet necklace, one was dull and clouded.

'Try and stay on the side of the damaged eye,' Etta panted, launching a violin as Felix flung a ski pole.

'Etta! Felix!' Mother shrieked behind them.

They swung around to see Etta's parents standing slack-jawed in the next section of the attic, staring at the enormous spider.

'Look out!' yelled Father, lunging forwards as Etta pulled Felix out of the path of the attacking spider.

Father reached them and wrapped his arms around both children, turning so his back was to the spider, protecting them both. He stumbled forward, gasping, and Etta knew the spider had scratched at him, snagging him with her claws.

Mother had reached the table of crystal balls, and she threw a large green one at the spider. The orb hit the creature square in the face, and began smoking, fogging up the attic and giving them some cover.

Father loosened his grip.

'Go, go!' he yelled, coughing as the smoke reached him. Mother threw another crystal ball.

'Fetch your grandmother!' she shouted. 'Tell her we need the ravens!'

Etta turned and ran straight into a cobweb hanging from the ceiling. She shrieked in surprise, scraping the dusty mess from her face.

'That's it!' she cried to Felix. 'The webs!'

'What webs? Quick, let's get your grandmother!' Felix tugged at Etta's jumper to bring her with him.

'The eels! The webs, the blue lightning!' Etta turned defiantly, looking across the attic. 'You fetch Grandmother, I'll wrap that monster in the eel webs.'

'No, Etta,' begged Felix. 'Please, come with me.'

Etta looked at her parents, surrounded by coloured smoke and flashes from the released crystals, battling against the spider she'd unleashed on the house.

'Go, Felix. Get the Eye safe, then find Grandmother,' Etta said forcefully.

She sidled around the edge of the attic, her eyes fixed on the dark webs that swagged the brick column above the trapdoor spider's lair. Those were the ones they'd thrown on their last trip up here, she could see the odd blue spark.

Etta was behind the spider now. She looked down at it from her position teetering on rotten old furniture. It was half obscured by the thick, coloured smoke from the crystal's escaping magic. She reached for the clumps of web, blue sparks crackling between them. She knew the eels wouldn't unravel from the webs without Felix holding on as well, but the electricity still sparked on the surface.

If I can throw the webs over her face, it should slow her long enough for us all to escape.

'Mary!' her father yelled below, and Etta looked to see the spider rearing up, about to drop on to her mother. Father leapt and got between them just in time.

Just in time for the spider to sink her fangs into his chest.

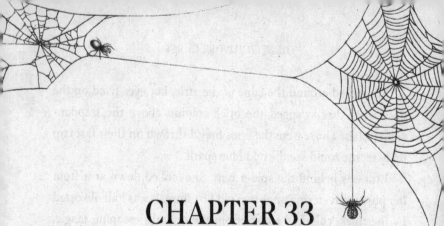

CHAPTER 33

MOTHER SCREAMED AS FATHER FELL, AND Etta threw the crackling heap of web from her hands. The webs fell over the spider's eyes. Confused, the spider staggered back, wiping at her stinging face with her feelers. Grandmother burst into the attic, with Felix close behind – Marin and several huge ravens swooping in above them.

Marin floated up until her back was on the ceiling, her hands over her mouth, shaking her head at the chaotic scene. Grandmother pointed, and the ravens dived at the spider. Etta knew they would aim for the eyes. The ancient creature would lose her sight entirely, maybe even die.

I did this. I went into the nest. I provoked her. This is all my fault.

The spider was retreating now, her body hunched down away from the ravens as she waved her front legs threateningly. Etta could sense the fight had gone out of her now. The attic was noisy, full of people, smoke, strange smells and bangs, electric shocks. The old spider was confused and wanted to go back to her quiet, safe nest.

Etta was trying not to look at where Mother knelt by Father. She didn't want to see the dark stain on the front of his shirt. Behind them, she saw Felix, rooted to the spot, his eyes and mouth wide.

A raven dropped towards the spider's face and Etta abruptly made her decision. She jumped down beside her, pulling the cobwebs away from the spider's eyes, ignoring the crackling across her fingers.

'Go,' she commanded, her gaze meeting the spider's. She tried to find a connection and felt the briefest feather-light tingle as she saw herself reflected in the spider's eyes. 'Go home. Rest. Sleep.'

The spider shook her influence off and Etta had to crack the cobweb like a whip, blue light flickering within it. The spider reared at her, flaring her fangs, venom dripping from them. The ravens circled and swooped at the spider's face again. She cowered, and rapidly retreated to her burrow, slamming the trapdoor firmly shut.

Dropping the cobweb and grabbing a jar, Etta scooped up some of the venom. Marin wheeled down from the ceiling, trembling and huddling close to her.

Felix pointed at one of the attic's odd windows.

'Etta! Look!' The ivy outside was thrashing madly at the window, the leaves scratching and squeaking against the glass.

Etta looked at her mother, who was holding Father tight. They'd unbuttoned his shirt and Grandmother was holding a compress over the wound. Mother sobbed as she smoothed his hair and beard down.

'She's upset, that's why the ivy's going crazy,' Etta told Felix, wondering why she felt so numb.

'Etta!' barked Grandmother. 'Call your spiders to weave a bandage over him, it'll stop the bleeding.'

Etta nodded and gulped a breath. She felt weak and her hands were shaking. Felix clasped them tightly with his.

'You can do this,' he said fiercely. 'You do it all the time.' He squeezed her hands tight. 'I'll help.'

Etta took a deep breath and as she exhaled, she found more connections than ever before. With Felix at her side, she felt their plea spread through the network of spiderwebs throughout the house, and the musical vibrations of the spiders as they rapidly answered. The first to arrive surrounded Grandmother and began spinning as fast as they could. Grandmother wadded the silk up and packed it into the puncture wounds. The silk absorbed the blood and stopped the bleeding.

'The venom is spreading, and I don't know what to treat it with.' Grandmother's cheeks had mottled red patches as she fussed and fretted over Father's wounds.

Etta ran and picked up the jar.

'I saved some venom for you.'

Grandmother sagged, looking so old and weary that Etta felt like she'd been winded.

'Thank you darling, but it'll take days to prepare.' She looked at Mother.

'Mary, we have to move him downstairs, try and keep him comfortable while we wait.'

The ivy scraped at the window as it continued to encircle the house.

'Help him,' Mother begged Grandmother.

'I will.' Grandmother's eyes were filled with tears. 'We'll try salt first. We'll try everything while the antivenom brews. Etta, ask the spiders to make a stretcher, let's get him downstairs to the infirmary.'

Tears streaming down her cheeks, Etta nodded. She and Felix grabbed some of the ski poles. They gripped each other's hands like a lifeline, and the spiders began to weave at their fastest.

Etta stared at the emerging stretcher without seeing it. Her ears had started ringing, a constant high-pitched sound, and there didn't seem to be enough air in the room. Felix seemed very far away. She was cold and shaking.

There was a tiny prick on Etta's wrist, and she looked to see a small jumping spider had given her a little nip. The noise of the attic came crashing back, the ivy, the ravens, her mother's crying.

And a thought, from the jumping spider that had snapped her back to herself, that she was a wanderer . . . And wanderers hunted down what they needed.

'Etta, Felix,' called Grandmother. 'Get the bigger spiders to help you take the stretcher down to the infirmary. Wake Viola, she can start boiling water.' She nodded across the attic, to where the crystal balls were out of control. 'Your mother and I have to deal with this, it's not safe to leave them loose. We'll have a fire on our hands in no time. Take the ravens with you, and any spiders. We need everyone out of here.'

Etta nodded compliantly, a different plan already forming. As Felix helped Grandmother move the stretcher under her father, Etta quietly scooped up what she needed.

They made their way awkwardly to the stairs, trying to keep

Father as level as possible, while Marin floated alongside.

'At least the bleeding's stopped,' Felix offered. He gave Etta a weak smile.

Etta checked they were out of Grandmother's sight, then a fiendish light lit her eyes.

'Finn!' she exclaimed. 'He's a healer! Do you remember those potion recipes in Benita's study? There were cures there. We'll take Father, we'll give them the Eye and beg for a cure.'

Felix looked at the nearest window, thick with roving leaves.

'Even if that were a good idea, I'm not sure how we'd get out of the house!'

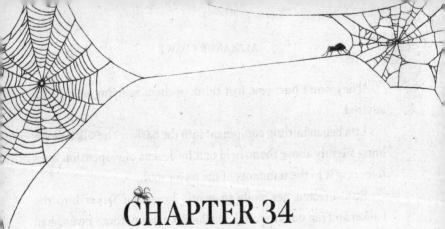

CHAPTER 34

GETTING FATHER ON TO THE ROOF WAS EASIER than expected. Etta's tree curled a branch down and lifted all three of them gently. Etta wrapped her arms around the bough.

'Thank you,' she whispered, her voice breaking.

From the roof they could see the ivy below, thick and restless, roving and wrapping around everything it could. Etta watched it covering every window and door with thick, impenetrable boughs.

'It's like Sleeping Beauty's castle,' Felix said, awestruck.

Etta marched across the roof after the wolf spiders, who carried her father's stretcher. Her bag of supplies bounced at her side.

'My father isn't sleeping for a hundred years,' she called. 'Come along, or the ivy will snare you.'

They reached the bat tower easily, the ivy concentrating on the parts of Stitchwort the family lived in. Felix was bent almost double as the bats swooped overhead. Marin gleefully swam up through the air to join in their looping flight.

'I prefer them asleep!' he complained.

ALEXANDRA DAWE

'They won't hurt you, just think of them as flying mice,' Etta advised.

Etta began hurling equipment into the basket. The silk balloon hung silently above them, held taut by dozens of suspension lines tethering it to the remnants of the tower roof.

Etta directed her wolfs to gently lower her father into the basket and fan out around the balloon. Grandmother's ravens had followed them up and were hopping about the platform, watching the spiders and bats with interest.

Etta spared the ravens a glance.

'Don't you dare,' she burst out harshly at them. One of the ravens ignored her and pecked at a passing bat, almost making a snack of it. Etta snapped, worry for her father overwhelming her. She ran at the birds, waving her arms. 'Shoo, go on, get away! I don't have time for you! Go! Or I'll have you all cocooned in silk!'

Cawing disparagingly at her, they flew up and circled the bat tower defiantly before landing on the roof of the ruined wing.

'Etta, I don't understand what we're doing here,' Felix said.

'We're going to fly out to sea and find Finn,' Etta replied firmly, gathering snow and jumping into the basket to pack it on to her father's injury.

Felix gawked at her.

'How? We haven't even tested out the fire yet! It might not work!'

'That's what these are for.' Etta patted her supplies bag. 'I grabbed them before we were sent out of the attic. Remember how we got swept up by the energy of the eels? They were trapped in the river, with the horses churning them up, and we got caught up in it and lifted into the air?'

Felix nodded. 'I'm not likely to ever forget it.'

'Well,' said Etta. 'If we release the eels into a contained space, like the balloon envelope, they'll lift the whole balloon for us.'

Felix looked at the balloon dubiously.

'That's a lot more weight than just us,' he began.

Etta held up a finger.

'Last time we started gathering the eels up, trying to stop them before they became too powerful. This time we won't. We'll let them rage. Now, are you coming with me or not?'

Felix climbed into the basket.

'Have you got the Eye?' Etta asked.

'Of course!' said Felix, patting his bag.

Etta suddenly flooded with doubt.

'What if they don't know the cures anymore? Ronan said they lost their garden and a lot of ingredients. What if they don't have the right ones?'

'It's alright, I'm sure they will,' soothed Felix. 'It's a good plan. Extreme, but good.'

Etta worried at her lower lip, then nodded decisively.

'Let's release the eels,' she said.

They stood side by side, linking hands. Etta drew a cobweb out of her bag and they held it up in the air between them. Lightning flared from end to end and Etta's hair started to float up and out, like a dandelion clock. She felt a tug, and her feet start to leave the ground.

'Now!' she cried, and they threw the cobweb up into the silk envelope.

Pulling the next cobweb from her satchel, they repeated the

process over and over again. The silk stretched tight, and the balloon began to bob and slide on the platform.

One of the eels snapped a head down out of the envelope, crackling electricity at them. They both ducked down, either side of Etta's father. Inside the balloon was a swirling, thundering cloud of black cobwebs – thick, thrashing eel bodies and blue lightning causing the silk canopy to flash with a blinding radiance.

'Cut the threads,' Etta called to the wolf spiders, and the tethers holding the balloon in place began to snap. The balloon lurched into the air and bobbed towards the outer wall of the bat tower.

'We need more height!' cried Felix. 'We're going to crash!'

Etta looked around frantically.

'It's father, he's too heavy. It was supposed to be a solo balloon! We'll have to jettison whatever we can.'

They threw out the stretcher poles, their empty bags and their boots. The basket hit the wall of the tower and they both fell down from the impact.

'It's still not enough,' moaned Felix. 'I'll go, you must stay with your father.' He braced his arms against the basket and readied himself to jump out when the balloon hit the wall again, dislodging a few bricks. With a long, creaking groan, a section of tower collapsed, the bricks cascading towards them.

Etta and Felix both screamed as the balloon spun out of control. Marin appeared, holding her position in the centre of the basket as it spiralled though her.

You need help

She said it decisively.

I can help . . . I will help

Raising her chin, she shot up into the envelope above them.

'Marin!' Etta called. 'Marin, don't go in there!'

The ghost girl was flying, pulling the eel storm with her and giving the balloon direction.

'Is she . . .' Felix leaned forwards, craning his neck to see better. 'Is she *herding* the eels?'

With a swaying lurch that flung them against the side of the basket they cleared the tower, accompanied by a swirling cloud of bats.

The balloon began to drag along the roof of the ruined wing, tiles scattering before them like a bow wave. Etta swung up on a rope and bellowed into the envelope for Marin to stop.

Felix was checking on her father. 'His pulse is strong, but his breathing seems weak.'

Etta nodded faintly. 'I think the venom is very close to his lungs.'

She looked over the side of the basket and waved to Marin to change their course, away from the house and grounds, taking them towards the bay.

Marin swung the balloon around and they began to lift.

The house fell away and the balloon slowly lifted into the sky above Stitchwort.

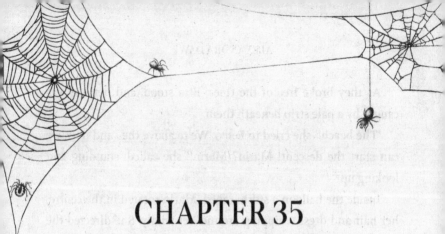

CHAPTER 35

FALLING INTO THE BASKET, LANDING BESIDE her father, Etta scrambled to her feet and looked out over the side.

It was so quiet up here. Her heart was still pounding and she could hear her own ragged breathing, but everything else was tranquil. She sighed with relief, feeling the tension drain from her body. Etta watched the ivy boiling over the house and the bats soaring past them as her breathing and heart rate returned to normal. The balloon climbed, revealing the beauty of the snow-covered countryside spread out beneath them.

Etta leaned over the edge of the basket, watching Grandmother's ravens lazily keeping pace with them. She sighed, knowing she couldn't just stand and admire the scenery. Turning, she crouched next to her father. Felix got the blankets out of the supplies chest and together they tucked Father in to keep him warm.

Felix put an arm around Etta's shoulders.

'There's no change, which is good. It means he's not getting any worse?' he suggested tentatively.

As they broke free of the trees, Etta stood, and her eye was caught by a pale strip beneath them.

'The beach!' she cried to Felix. 'We're above the sand now, we can start the descent! Marin? Marin!' she called, standing and looking up.

Inside the balloon a storm raged. Marin rotated in the centre, her hair and dress whipping around her wildly. She directed the shoal of eels as they raced around the perimeter, so fast they were a blur. Their electric discharges crackled from the top of the envelope right down to the opening with a bang. Etta jumped back in surprise.

Felix was still kneeling beside her father, but the noise alerted him as well. He pulled Etta down, further away from the cracking lightning.

'Etta, I think there's enough power in there now. How do we make it stop?'

Etta shook her head, transfixed by the hurricane of eels.

'I . . . I don't know, I didn't think it would get so strong.' She watched the lightning rage around the inside of the silk dome, furiously looking for a way out. The next bolt snaked down towards them, wrapping around the ropes that tied the basket to the balloon. The ropes started smoking, the burning smell causing Etta's eyes to water.

'Does spider silk burn?' asked Felix anxiously, as he squinted up at the whirring blue glow.

'Not exactly . . .' Etta looked over the basket to see how high up they were. To her relief they were over the sea now. 'It doesn't burst into flames or anything. It just sort of . . . melts.'

'Melts?' Felix echoed, flatly.

'Marin!' yelled Etta, hoping the ghost could hear her. 'We're here, go lower.'

Etta was still looking up when she saw it. A dark spot on a section of the silk envelope. It took a moment for her to work out it wasn't a spreading black stain, but a growing hole. A hole in the silk, open to the night sky. As she watched, an eel slithered its way out through it and the balloon sagged.

'Marin! We have to stop it!' Etta shouted, cold panic sweeping across her as she saw other holes opening up, tearing through the smoking silk faster and faster. More eels spilled out and the deflating balloon plummeted towards the freezing ocean.

Marin flew past them, arching out of the canopy and diving like a seabird after a fish. She sliced into the water like a sword, the eels following. Etta clutched at Felix and pointed as a gentleman with a bristling moustache and round glasses fell past, his knees drawn up to his chest and holding his nose.

'It's Harold!' Etta yelled.

With an enormous splash the balloon hit the sea, drenching them both with icy water.

'Quick,' Etta said to Felix. 'Push the silk away.'

The envelope was collapsing on top of them as it disintegrated, threatening to trap them inside the basket as it sank into the freezing sea. The ravens swooped around, snapping and tugging at the silk, trying to keep it off them.

Etta and Felix ran to look over the side of the basket, causing it to tip. Etta squealed as her father slumped lower, his chin falling into the water. She knelt beside him, lifting his head as gently as she could.

'We're sinking!' Felix called.

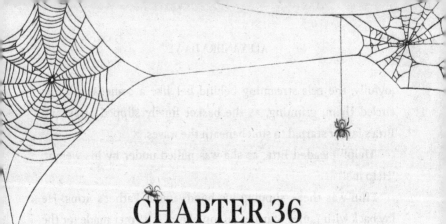

CHAPTER 36

'**W**E CAN SEE THAT,' CAME AERWYNNA'S voice. 'What do you think you're doing?'

'It's the twins!' Etta cried joyously to Felix. 'We have the Eye!' she called back to Aerwynna, kneeling in the rising water. 'But my father is hurt, we need your help.'

Felix pulled out the Eye and, leaning over the edge of the basket, held it up for the twins to see.

'Give it to me!' Aerwynna demanded, holding her webbed hands out to catch it.

'Can you heal Etta's father?' Felix pleaded, looking from her to Finn.

'Felix!' Etta called. Her father was floating now, as the basket slipped further beneath the waves. Felix put the Eye back in his satchel as he crouched to help her. The ravens took off, flying across the water back to the house.

'This is ridiculous,' Aerwynna snapped. 'We cannot have a conversation like this.'

Marin arced up out of the water, laughing and spinning

joyfully, the eels streaming behind her like a comet's tail. She circled them, grinning, as the basket finally slipped away and Etta's father started to sink beneath the waves.

'Help!' pleaded Etta, as she was pulled under by his weight. 'Help me!'

Finn was there, slipping his hands under Father's arms. He lay back with James Starling on top of him. The mer made for the shore, his golden tail propelling him far quicker than any human could swim.

Etta and Felix doggy paddled on the spot, Etta coughing as seawater went into her mouth.

Aerwynna was staring at Marin, frolicking though the sea with the eels.

'You found her skin as well?' she looked at them with disbelief etched all over her face. 'Why isn't she in her proper form then?'

Etta was tiring, the water was so cold.

She coughed again. 'We've found it, we just haven't quite gotten it back to her yet. We will though, I promise.'

Aerwynna watched Marin skimming over the waves.

'You two are full of surprises!'

Felix's teeth were chattering so hard he couldn't even speak, but he held out the bag with the Eye in.

Aerwynna took the satchel and withdrew the gleaming pearl, her eyes alight and her face truly happy for the first time since they'd met her.

'It's beautiful,' she whispered. She seemed to be listening. 'I can feel it, it's so happy to be back in the sea!' She hugged the pearl tight to her chest and spun around in the water.

'Aerwynna, please,' Etta begged. 'We're freezing and our clothes are so heavy.'

Marin swooped down.

Help them

She glared at Aerwynna, who scowled at her.

'Fine,' Aerwynna huffed. 'As you're Ronan's family. I'll lead them back to shore.'

Cradling the Eye in one arm, Aerwynna began to swim backwards. Etta felt the waves nudge and caress her, gently pushing her and Felix towards the shore. Marin hovered above, and the eels rippled up and down through the waves on either side of them.

Aerwynna stopped at an outcrop of rocks that jutted out, where Finn waited with Etta's father.

Etta swam weakly across.

'Can you help my father? He was bitten by a huge spider.'

Finn shook his head.

'I can't get a cure made fast enough. He's weak, his breathing's bad.'

He turned to his sister, cradling the Eye like a baby seal pup.

'Wynn, can you do something?'

She snorted.

'He wasn't poisoned with seawater, was he? I only have power over water.'

Finn frowned. The snow had been washed off Etta's father's chest, revealing how his veins were darkening as the venom spread out from the puncture wounds. 'You have the Eye now, Wynn. There's a lot of water in blood, and probably in venom. Maybe

using the Eye, you can separate it all out and just keep the right liquids in him.'

Aerwynna glowered at him.

'You'd be the first siren to have done such a thing – separated out blood and venom,' Finn wheedled. 'Everyone would want to know how you did it. The Elders would want to carve the knowledge in the rocks for future generations.'

Aerwynna flicked her hair over her shoulder and narrowed her eyes at him.

'I know you're only flattering me to get what you want.'

'You always were smarter than me,' Finn grinned.

'Fine,' she snapped. 'I'll try.' She looked at Etta, clinging on to her father's hand as it trailed in the water. 'You'd better sit up there and hold on to him. I've never done this before. I don't know if it'll work.'

Aerwynna held the Eye in both hands, and softly began her siren song. Her magic began to build, tiny glowing tendrils of coral light twining around her fingers. As they reached the Eye, the tendrils flared, growing rapidly, becoming thicker and longer. Aerwynna's eyebrows shot up but she kept on singing, directing it towards her patient.

The magic rolled over Father like a wave, bathing him in a coral glow. As it reached the wound on his chest, Finn whispered to Etta.

'Take the dressings off!'

Etta quickly removed the spiderwebs. She couldn't bear to look at the punctures in Father's chest, stained berry black by venom, but the magic pooled in them and the lines of poison spreading under his skin changed colour. The map of veins now glowed a pure, rosy hue.

Aerwynna changed her song and the glow retreated, the magic withdrawing from the wounds and closing them up as it left.

'Father,' Etta sobbed, squeezing his arm.

'Shhh, give him a minute,' advised Finn.

Aerwynna held the Eye in one hand, while teasing her magic across the fingers of her other hand. The colours were slowly separating out, the coral winding back into her, leaving a dark bead hanging in the air.

'Is that the venom?' Etta asked.

Aerwynna nodded.

'The venom, and some of your father's blood.' She wiggled her fingers and it shimmered. 'What would you like to do with it?'

Etta pulled a face.

'Get rid of it so it can't hurt anyone else!' she instructed.

Aerwynna danced it across the waves until it reached the shore. With a flick of her fingers the ball of venom shattered on the cliffs, leaving a dark stain.

Father groaned and tried to sit up. Finn reached up and supported him as Etta and Felix helped.

'Etta!' Father hugged her close, his grip far weaker than normal. 'Are you hurt, where did that spider go?' He looked around and saw he was on the beach.

'What's happening? Why are we here? The curse! We have to get back indoors!' He tried to stand but couldn't manage it, and collapsed on one knee, seeing Finn and Aerwynna for the first time. He stared at them.

Aerwynna frowned at Etta.

'This curse of yours, it does seem problematic. The first time we met, you were almost drowned – trapped by a tide that rose far too high and fast to have been natural.'

Father slowly turned his head to stare at Etta, who didn't meet his gaze.

'Now you've been surrounded by your own personal lightning storm, crashed into the sea, and nearly drowned again!' She rotated the Eye in her hands. 'I'm not sure I entirely believe in this curse, but you do seem to attract trouble. I wonder if I can do something about that . . .'

Aerwynna rested the Eye on the rocks and looked into it thoughtfully, almost as if they were in conversation. Then she began to murmur a low chant. The words rose to a crescendo, her magic dancing out of her fingertips as wide pale ribbons of light. They encircled the rocks and the beach, weaving around the bay and the sea caves.

'There.' Aerwynna looked pleased with herself. 'I've protected the beach, the caves and the cliffs. You'll hopefully get into less trouble now.'

'I doubt it,' muttered Father. He held his hand out to Aerwynna. 'It's very nice to meet you, I'm James Starling. I understand I have you to thank for rescuing us, although I confess to having no idea how we got here.'

As Finn launched into an animated retelling of the balloon lurching over the cliffs towards the ocean, Etta looked at Felix. He was staring at the shore.

Following his gaze, she realised Viola was standing there, with Marin and the ghost eels orbiting her as though she were the sun.

CHAPTER 37

THE SUN WAS RISING NOW, A ROSY GLOW creeping over the waves. The sea sparkled where the light touched it.

The beach was deserted, the pale sand smooth and undisturbed. The village sat amongst the hills on the south side of the bay, the rocks and cliffs behind them to the north and west. Standing on the rocks with her father and Felix, Etta looked up to the treetops, but Stitchwort was well hidden from her here.

Etta inhaled the salt air and marvelled at the fresh beauty of the spring beach, cold though it was. Aerwynna had dried their clothes at least. The sound of the waves washing onto the shore was soothing. A strong breeze buffeted them.

Felix linked arms with Etta, and they began to walk across the rocks to where Viola waited at the water's edge.

'Over there,' Felix said, pointing. There were seals among the rocks to their left, gazing at the children with their boundless, deep eyes. As Etta turned back to look out to sea again, she saw more seal heads bob up in the ocean before them.

The two children held on tight to each other's arms, like anchors against the world. They carefully climbed across the slimy, slippery stones. There were little waterfalls and streams in between the bigger rocks.

Etta was enthralled by everything she saw. This was going to be a wonderful place to explore now that Aerwynna had made it safe for them.

They were on the beach now. They trudged on, the sand hard and damp beneath their feet. Etta turned her head, neck prickling as she sensed eyes on her, to see Ronan crossing towards them, his spotted sealskin open at the throat, the hood back.

'You found the Mermaid's Eye?' he asked incredulously. 'I saw everything.'

'We found the Eye,' confirmed Felix simply, as he beamed from ear to ear.

'And my great-great-grandmother's sealskin?' asked Ronan eagerly.

Felix looked past him, to where Viola still waited, hugging something close to her body. Etta smiled to herself; she could think of only one reason why Marin would be circling Viola, only one way the ghost would have been able to leave Stitchwort's grounds.

'Mama?' Felix asked gently.

'I'm so sorry,' Viola whispered. 'I was wrong about everything. We never really know when disaster's going to strike next, do we?'

'That's cheerful, thanks Mama,' Felix replied, with a wry smile.

Viola laughed.

'You know what I mean, *schatje*. I brought us here thinking this would be a place where we could hide from the world and be safe. And we found a family who were safe and hiding from the world, who were suffering because of that.' She sighed. 'We're not safe anywhere. If it's not the war nipping at our heels then it's crumbling ruins, or giant spiders, or ghost eels.' She watched the eels as they followed Marin's flight. She shook her head. 'Hiding isn't living. What if you'd drowned when that balloon crashed? What if those crystals had burnt the house down and killed us all?'

'Very cheerful, Auntie Vi,' added Etta.

'I'm serious,' Viola said sternly. 'I took this away from you to keep us safe.' She shook out the bundle, revealing the sealskin. There was no sign of paint, or damage, and the velvet fur gleamed softly.

'How did you . . . ?' breathed Felix.

'Grandmother Starling got started on it as soon as I dragged you both off to the kitchen last night. When I'd calmed down, I went and helped her. There were a few tiny holes, but with my talent for sewing and a little spider thread it's as though it were never torn in the first place. The skin is healed. It's fragile, but it's whole. And if the house had burnt down it might have been destroyed, lost forever. That spirit would never have her freedom.

'I had no right to take this. I saw that selkie help you fly your balloon, and I saw those merfolk rescue you and heal James.' She held the sealskin out to them.

Etta and Felix proudly held the skin out for Ronan to see. The wind caught it and it felt for a moment as though the skin itself strained towards the sea, longing for freedom.

'I can't believe it,' said Ronan. 'I just can't believe that you did it! This is incredible!' His smile was joyous, and infectious – and

Etta and Felix couldn't help but smile too.

'Here, take it,' said Felix, holding the skin towards him. 'Return it to the sea, let Marin have her true form back.'

'I can't,' said Ronan seriously, taking a step back and holding his hands up and away from the skin. 'That's not how it works with selkies. The one who causes the injury has to be the one to fix it. One of your blood inflicted this pain and stole her away from the sea, so one of yours must end the pain and return her. I still scarce believe you did it though!' He couldn't stop grinning as the three of them turned to the water's edge.

Marin was waiting there. Etta could see the sunrise through her, could see the waiting seals through the ghost's translucent form.

'So . . . what do we do now?' Etta asked Ronan uncertainly.

'Walk out into the water, as far as you can, and lower the skin in,' he advised calmly. 'Then let the ocean do the rest.'

The pelt felt heavier now. Back in the house it had felt light and dry, fragile, like very old paper. But here, close to the sea, the selkie's skin felt dense, more vital, warm and almost alive. Etta and Felix held it reverently between them. Etta took a deep breath and stepped into the ocean. She gasped in shock as the numbing tide washed over her feet and up to her ankles.

'It's FREEZING!' Etta yelped, dancing on the spot, her toes curled up. She took a few more steps, gasping with the cold. 'I just got dry as well,' she complained.

When they were thigh-deep, Etta's dress floating on the surface, she looked nervously over her shoulder. Ronan was just a few steps behind, but Marin was still ashore.

'A little deeper,' murmured Ronan.

Etta gave him a hard glare, her face was white with cold and her lips were now a dark mauve. Her wild hair whipped around in the wind. She could hear Felix's teeth chattering.

'Sorry,' Ronan whispered, but smirked a little, ruining it. 'The sea isn't cold to us.'

Etta and Felix held the skin up for all of the seals surrounding them to see. It glowed in the sunlight as they laid it down on the surface of the water. Etta's fingers tingled strangely. There came a peculiar sort of pulse, then she felt a deep sigh as she turned to meet Marin's eyes. The ghost smiled and gracefully glided forwards into the water.

Both the ghost and the sealskin shone with a shimmering silver outline. Marin swam through the water towards her floating skin, a rapidly undulating silver streak. Ghost and pelt whirled until they blurred and became a beautiful, glowing, silver seal. She bobbed her head up out of the water and barked joyously. All the other seals barked in response. Etta held out her hand to stroke the silver seal, but her touch passed right through.

'I'm so sorry,' she whispered, a tear rolling down her cheek.

'You're forgiven,' said Ronan wryly, unable to take his eyes from the rippling shape of the silver seal as she swam joyously through the waves.

All around them were writhing seal bodies, slipping gracefully past each other, weaving a celebration. Ronan started pulling the hood of his own skin up.

'Thank you,' he said simply. 'From all of us.'

He flashed a dazzling smile, covered his face and ducked down under the water. Then a beautiful young seal arched up and dived into the waves. The writhing mass of joyful seals moved further out into the sparkling sea. The celebration was so merry that Felix and Etta stood watching until they couldn't see them anymore.

Etta and Felix held each other up as they laboriously waded back to the shore and saw their whole family waiting on the beach for them. When they reached the shallows they broke into a run, tripping and splashing out of the sea to tell them everything.

Grandmother and Mother had brought flasks of hot tea, towels and blankets. Ronald was making a fire. There were even warm, dry clothes for them. Soon Etta and Felix were swaddled in blankets, hugging their hot drinks, and feeling triumphant and cosy.

'You and I have never been to the seaside before,' Mother reminded Etta. 'Would you walk with me?'

They walked together, barefoot in spite of the cold, feeling sand between their toes and collecting shells.

'Don't go thinking you're not in a whole world of trouble, young lady,' Mother scolded. 'But for now, we're all so grateful to be alive, you're getting a temporary reprieve. However, tomorrow you and Felix are telling us absolutely everything that you've been doing.' She tried to look stern but squealed with delight when she saw her first rock pool.

Our first ever day out at the seaside.

Etta rested, taking in the wondrous glory of every new sight, smell and sound. She and Felix were soon running up and down, shouting and playing. Felix did cartwheels along the sand.

Later, as the tide came back in, merfolk and selkies made their way to meet the family. The selkies, in shades of grey and brown, shyly watched from a safe distance, but the golden, glittering mer were bolder and came to introduce themselves. Ronald disappeared up the old path to the house and soon returned with a fiddle. Before too much longer, James vanished and came back with boxes of food. Etta and Felix gathered driftwood to make a fire, which Grandfather impressively ignited with a flick of his bony fingers. He laughed and promised to teach the trick to Etta and Felix.

'It's an easy little spell, quite useful though. If the air will listen to you!'

Etta sat back to drink in the scene. Ronald was playing the most amazing music, like nothing she'd ever heard before. Her father was offering biscuits around the rock pools where the mer swayed to the melody. Her grandparents were in deep discussion with an elderly mer lady, with more jewels even than Finn, who was holding the Eye in her webbed fingers. Mother, Viola and Felix were laughing nearby as Viola taught Mother the steps to a dance she called the Lindy Hop.

Mother's going to have to start wearing trousers, Etta thought, watching her struggle with the dance steps.

Some of the mer had brought along their own instruments, and as Ronald finished his tune they began to play one of their own. Felix came and flopped down beside Etta.

'Phew! I haven't danced in ages!' he puffed, a little out of breath.

'You're really good, can you teach me?' asked Etta.

'Absolutely,' grinned Felix. 'And what will you teach me?' he laughed.

Etta chewed on some gingerbread thoughtfully.

'Would you like to help me catapult a skeleton off the roof? It's scientific.'

As Felix lay back on the sand and laughed, Etta swallowed the last mouthful of her biscuit, looking at all the activity on the beach.

'Everything is going to change,' she whispered gleefully.

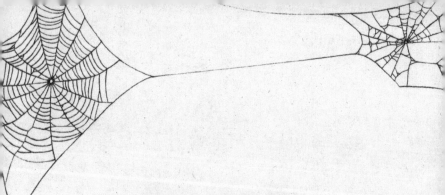

EPILOGUE

STITCHWORT STOOD QUIET AND EMPTY. FOR the first time in decades, there wasn't a single person at home. The kitchen fire was burning low, the library fire merely embers now. The house was dark and silent in the gathering gloom.

In a shadowy alcove in the ruined wing hung the bleak painting of Stitchwort house, looking grim and desolate. A tiny light glowed for a moment in one of the gaunt, painted windows, and then faded. It reappeared, then faded again, the movement as though someone walked from room to room with a candle.

Steadily getting closer to the front door.

ACKNOWLEDGEMENTS

I DIDN'T MEAN TO WRITE A BOOK. WHAT STARTED as a few notes about Victorian science and society, for drawing ideas, grew and grew until it was 40,000 words long.

As I researched more I became fascinated with the plant hunters of the 17th and 18th centuries. I read *100 Flowers and How They Got Their Names* by Diana Wells. The wild adventures, near-death experiences and untimely demises of these explorers shaped an idea: the last remaining members of a cursed family only safe within their own boundary wall. The rest of the world had continued while they were still frozen in the 1800s, too afraid to leave. I carried on writing, until I thought it was finished (it wasn't, as it turned out) and I sent it out into the world.

I was, and still am, stunned when Lauren Gardner phoned me. I am enormously grateful to everyone at Bell Lomax Moreton, especially Lauren, Justine and Julie, for the advice and encouragement you offered to help me give that rambling mess some much needed direction. With a pandemic and homeschooling in the middle, this has been a long time coming!

Thank you also to Hazel at UcLan, for giving Etta and Felix a home. To Nicki for the brilliant proofreading, and finding the missing paragraph! And Becky, for absolutely incredible book design – I can't believe how wonderful you've made every page look.

Most of all, thank you to my incredible editor Tilda, who has been so kind and patient when I was late and lost. I'm sorry I ruined your holiday by making you know too much about spiders.

Thank you also to all the wonderful individuals, groups and organisations who make so much information accessible online. I knew very little about spiders when I began this journey, and I only hope I've not made too many glaring mistakes. A special thanks to John Baker of the British Balloon Museum and Library, for his information and diagrams.

I am very fortunate to have such wonderful friends: Genna, Sarah, Ruth, Ali and Laura, who make me laugh until I ache. Barri and Sarah – extra thanks to Sarah for translating the Grey family's words into Dutch, and helping with my copy-editing woes. Chris, for drawing Stitchwort when the roof angles overwhelmed me. Verity, for being there for anything and everything, from parenting to interior design. And Toni, who is with me in the studio every day, for every single Whatsapp and shared hot choc.

For my parents, who gifted me with a love of reading and have always bought me books. I hope you enjoy reading this one.

Finally, to my wonderful husband Pete – there aren't words for all the support you give me.

And my beautiful children, Rowan and Jacob.

(Jacob, I swear, if you still won't read it now . . .)

ABOUT THE AUTHOR

ALEXANDRA DAWE WAS BORN IN LIVERPOOL, and grew up with the sea at the end of her road. She has always loved to read and draw, especially folklore, fantasy and fairy tales. Seeing the movie *Labyrinth* as a teenager led her to work as a props and model maker in Shepperton and Pinewood studios. Alexandra has had lots of other jobs including being a terrible waitress, picture framing, and as an editor at Palgrave Macmillan.

Alexandra now lives in Devon with her husband, children, the best ever dog, two cats, and several elderly chickens. She loves tea, chocolate, and being at the seaside.

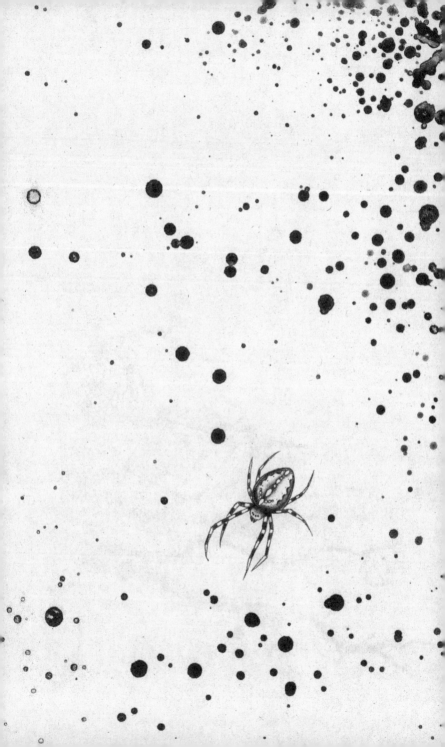

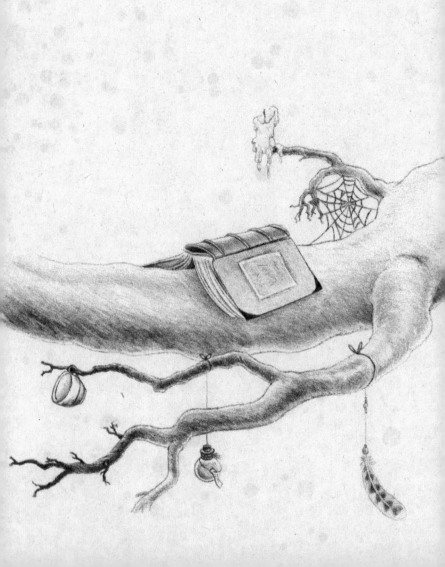